Frederick The Great And His Family
A Historical Novel
Book II

by

L. Mühlbach

Frederick The Great And His Family
A Historical Novel
Book II
by L. Mühlbach

Copyright © 2024

All Rights reserved.

No part of this publication may be reproduced, stored in a retrieval system, or transmitted in any form or by any means, electronic, mechanical, photocopying or Otherwise, without the written permission of the publisher.
The author/editor asserts the moral right to be identified as the author/editor of this work.

ISBN: 978-93-62204-67-7

Published by

DOUBLE 9 BOOKS

2/13-B, Ansari Road
Daryaganj, New Delhi – 110002
info@double9books.com
www.double9books.com
Tel. 011-40042856

This book is under public domain

ABOUT THE AUTHOR

Luise Muhlbach, born Clara Maria Regina Muller on January 2, 1814, in Neubrandenburg, Germany, was a renowned German writer acclaimed for her historical fiction. Writing under the pseudonym Luise Muhlbach, she captivated readers with vivid narratives that brought history to life. Despite a relatively short-lived period of popularity, her works continue to resonate with audiences. Born to Friedrich Andreas Müller and Friederika Müller (nee Strübing), Clara displayed early literary talent that flourished into a prolific career. Her most famous novel, "Frederick the Great and His Court" (German: Friedrich der Grosse und sein Hof), stands as a testament to her narrative prowess. This and many other works were translated into English, broadening her reach and influence. Muhlbach's storytelling skill lay in her ability to intertwine historical accuracy with compelling characters and plotlines, transporting readers to different epochs with ease. Through her writing, she illuminated the complexities of bygone eras, offering insights into the lives of prominent figures and the societies they inhabited. Though she passed away on September 26, 1873, in Berlin, Muhlbach's literary legacy endures, ensuring that her contributions to the genre of historical fiction remain cherished and celebrated by generations of readers worldwide.

CONTENTS

CHAPTER I
THE UNHAPPY NEWS

The Princess Amelia was alone in her room. She was stretched upon a sofa, lost in deep thought; her eyes were raised to heaven, and her lips trembled; from time to time they murmured a word of complaint or of entreaty.

Amelia was ill. She had been ill since that unhappy day in which she intentionally destroyed her beauty to save herself from a hated marriage. *[Footnote: See "Berlin and Sans-Souci."]* Her eyes had never recovered their glance or early fire; they were always inflamed and veiled by tears. Her voice had lost its metallic ring and youthful freshness; it sounded from her aching and hollow chest like sighs from a lonely grave.

Severe pain from time to time tortured her whole body, and contracted her limbs with agonizing cramps. She had the appearance of a woman of sixty years of age, who was tottering to the grave.

In this crushed and trembling body dwelt a strong, powerful, healthy soul; this shrunken, contracted bosom was animated by a youthful, ardent, passionate heart. This heart had consecrated itself to the love of its early years with an obstinate and feverish power.

In wild defiance against her fate, Amelia had sworn never to yield, never to break faith; to bear all, to suffer all for her love, and to press onward with unshaken resignation but never-failing courage through the storms and agonies of a desolate, misunderstood, and wretched existence. She was a martyr to her birth and her love; she accepted this martyrdom with defiant self-reliance and joyful resignation.

Years had passed since she had seen Trenck, but she loved him still! She knew he had not guarded the faith they had mutually sworn with the constancy that she had religiously maintained; but she loved him still! She had solemnly sworn to her brother to give up the foolish and fantastic wish of becoming the wife of Trenck; but she loved him still! She might not live for him, but she would suffer for him; she could not give him her hand, but she could consecrate thought and soul to him. In imagination she was his, only his; he had a holy, an imperishable right to her. Had she not sworn, in the presence of God, to be his through life down to the borders of the grave? Truly, no priest had blessed them; God had been their priest, and had united them. There had been no mortal witness to their solemn oaths, but the pure stars were present—with their sparkling, loving eyes they had looked down and listened to the vows she had exchanged with Trenck. She was therefore his—his eternally! He had a sacred claim upon her constancy, her love, her forbearance, and her forgiveness. If Trenck had wandered from his faith, she dared not follow his example; she must be ever ready to listen to his call, and give him the aid he required.

Amelia's love was her religion, her life's strength, her life's object; it was a talisman to protect and give strength in time of need. She would have died without it; she lived and struggled with her grief only for his sake.

This was a wretched, joyless existence—a never-ending martyrdom, a never-ceasing contest. Amelia stood alone and unloved in her family, feared and avoided by all the merry, thoughtless, pleasure seeking circle. In her sad presence they shuddered involuntarily and felt chilled, as by a blast from the grave. She was an object of distrust and weariness to her companions and servants, an object of love and frank affection to no one.

Mademoiselle Ernestine von Haak had alone remained true to her; but she had married, and gone far away with her husband. Princess Amelia was now alone; there was no one to whom she could express her sorrow and her fears; no one who understood her suppressed agony, or who spoke one word of consolation or sympathy to her broken heart.

She was alone in the world, and the consciousness of this steeled her strength, and made an impenetrable shield for her wearied soul. She gave herself up entirely to her thoughts and dreams. She lived a strange, enchanted, double life and twofold existence. Outwardly, she was old, crushed, ill; her interior life was young, fresh, glowing, and energetic, endowed with unshaken power, and tempered in the fire of her great grief. Amelia lay upon the divan and looked dreamily toward heaven. A strange and unaccountable presentiment was upon her; she trembled with mysterious forebodings. She had always felt thus when any new misfortunes were about to befall Trenck. It seemed as if her soul was bound to his, and by means of an electric current she felt the blow in the same moment that it fell upon him.

The princess believed in these presentiments. She had faith in dreams and prophecies, as do all those unhappy beings to whom fate has denied real happiness, and who seek wildly in fantastic visions for compensation. She loved, therefore, to look into the future through fortune-tellers and dark oracles, and thus prepare herself for the sad events which lay before her. The day before, the renowned astrologer Pfannenstein had warned her of approaching peril; he declared that a cloud of tears was in the act of bursting upon her! Princess Amelia believed in his words, and waited with a bold, resolved spirit for the breaking of the cloud, whose gray veil she already felt to be round about her.

These sad thoughts were interrupted by a light knock upon the door, and her maid entered and announced that the master of ceremonies, Baron Pollnitz, craved an audience.

Amelia shuddered, but roused herself quickly. "Let him enter!" she said, hastily. The short moment of expectation seemed an eternity of anguish. She pressed her hands upon her heart, to still its stormy beatings; she looked with staring, wide-opened eyes toward the door through which Pollnitz must enter, and she shuddered as she looked upon the ever-smiling, immovable face of the courtier, who now entered her boudoir, with Mademoiselle von Marwitz at his side.

"Do you know, Pollnitz," said she, in a rough, imperious tone—"do you know I believe your face is not flesh and blood, but hewn from stone; or, at least, one day it was petrified? Perhaps the fatal hour struck one day, just as you were laughing over some of your villainies, and your smile was turned to stone as a judgment. I shall know this look as long as I live; it is ever most clearly marked upon your visage, when you have some misfortune to announce."

"Then this stony smile must have but little expression to-day, for I do not come as a messenger of evil tidings; but if your royal highness will allow me to say so, as a sort of postillon d'amour."

Amelia shrank back for a moment, gave one glance toward Mademoiselle von Marwitz, whom she knew full well to be the watchful spy of her mother, and whose daily duty it was to relate to the queen-mother every thing which took place in the apartment of the princess. She knew that every word and look of Pollnitz was examined with the strictest attention.

Pollnitz, however, spoke on with cool self-possession:

"You look astonished, princess; it perhaps appears to you that this impassive face is little suited to the role of postillon d'amour, and yet that is my position, and I ask your highness's permission to make known my errand."

"I refuse your request," said Amelia, roughly; "I have nothing to do with Love, and find his godship as old and dull as the messenger he has sent me. Go back, then, to your blind god, and tell him that my ears are deaf to his love greeting, and the screeching of the raven is more melodious than the tenderest words a Pollnitz can utter."

The princess said this in her most repulsive tone. She was accustomed to shield herself in this rude manner from all approach or contact, and, indeed, she attained her object. She was feared and avoided. Her witty bon mots and stinging jests were repeated and merrily laughed over, but the world knew that she scattered her sarcasms far and wide, in order to secure her isolation; to banish every one from her presence, so that none might hear her sighs, or read her sad history in her countenance.

"And yet, princess, I must still implore a hearing," said he, with imperturbable good-humor; "if my voice is rough as the raven's, your royal highness must feed me with sugar, and it will become soft and tender as an innocent maiden's."

"I think a few ducats would be better for your case," said Amelia; "a Pollnitz is not to be won with sweets, but for gold he would follow the devil to the lower regions."

"You are right, princess; I do not wish to go to heaven, but be low; there I am certain to find the best and most interesting society. The genial people are all born devils, and your highness has ever confessed that I am genial. Then let it be so! I will accept the ducats which your royal highness think good for me, and now allow me to discharge my duty. I come as the messenger of Prince Henry: He sends his heart-felt greetings to his royal sister, and begs that she will do him the honor to attend fete at Rheinsberg, which will take place in eight days."

"Has the master of ceremonies of the king become the fourrier of Prince Henry?" said Amelia.

"No, princess; I occasionally and accidentally perform the function of a fourrier. This invitation was not my principal object to-day."

"I knew it," said Amelia, ironically. "My brother Henry does not love me well enough to invite me to this fete, if he had not some other object to attain. Well, what does Prince Henry wish?"

"A small favor, your royal highness; he wishes, on the birthday of his wife, to have Voltaire's 'Rome Sauvee' given by the French tragedians. Some years since your highness had a great triumph in this piece. The prince remembers that Voltaire prepared the role of Aurelia especially for you, with changes and additions, and he entreats you, through me, the temporary Directeur des spectacles de Rheinsberg, to lend him this role for the use of his performer."

"Why does not my brother rather entreat me to take this part myself?" said Amelia, in cruel mockery over herself. "It appears to me I could look the part of Aurelia, and my soft, flute-like voice would make a powerful impression upon the public. It is cruel of Prince Henry to demand this role of me; it might be inferred that he thought I had become old and ugly."

"Not so, your highness; the tragedy is to be performed on this occasion by public actors, and not by amateurs."

"You are right," said Amelia, suddenly becoming grave; "at that time we were amateurs, lovers of the drama; our dreams are over—we live in realities now."

"Mademoiselle von Marwitz, have the goodness to bring the manuscript my brother wishes; it is partly written by Voltaire's own hand. You will find it in the bureau in my dressing-room."

Mademoiselle Marwitz withdrew to get the manuscript; as she left the room, she looked back suspiciously at Pollnitz and, as if by accident, left the door open which led to the dressing-room.

Mademoiselle Marwitz had scarcely disappeared, before Pollnitz sprang forward, with youthful agility, and closed the door.

"Princess, this commission of Prince Henry's was only a pretext. I took this order from the princess's maitre d'hotel in order to approach your highness unnoticed, and to get rid of the watchful eyes of your Marwitz. Now listen well; Weingarten, the Austrian secretary of Legation, was with me to-day."

"Ah, Weingarten," murmured the princess, tremblingly; "he gave you a letter for me; quick, quick, give it to me."

"No, he gave me no letter; it appears that he, who formerly sent letters, is no longer in the condition to do so."

"He is dead!" cried Amelia with horror, and sank back as if struck by lightning.

"No, princess, he is not dead, but in great danger. It appears that Weingarten is in great need of money; for a hundred louis d'or, which I promised him, he confided to me that Trenck's enemies had excited the suspicions of the king against him, and declared that Trenck had designs against the life of Frederick."

"The miserable liars and slanderers!" cried Amelia, contemptuously.

"The king, as it appears, believes in these charges; he has written to his resident minister to demand of the senate of Dantzic the delivery of Trenck."

"Trenck is not in Dantzic, but in Vienna."

"He is in Dantzic—or, rather, he was there."

"And now?"

"Now," said Pollnitz, solemnly, "he is on the way to Konigsberg; from that point he will be transported to some other fortress; first, however, he will be brought to Berlin."

The unhappy princess uttered a shriek, which sounded like a wild death-cry. "He is, then, a prisoner?"

"Yes; but, on his way to prison, so long as he does not cross the threshold of the fortress, it is possible to deliver him. Weingarten, who, it appears to me, is much devoted to your highness, has drawn for me the plan of the route, Trenck is to take. Here it is." He handed the princess a small piece of paper, which she seized with trembling hands, and read hastily.

"He comes through Coslin," said she, joyfully; "that gives a chance of safety in Coslin! The Duke of Wurtemberg, the friend of my youthful days, is in Coslin; he will assist me. Pollnitz, quick, quick, find me a courier who will carry a letter to the duke for me without delay."

"That will be difficult, if not impossible," said Pollnitz, thoughtfully.

Amelia sprang from her seat; her eyes had the old fire, her features their youthful expression and elasticity.

The power and ardor of her soul overcame the weakness of her body; it found energy and strength.

"Well, then," said she, decisively, and even her voice was firm and soft, "I will go myself; and woe to him who dares withhold me! I have been ordered to take sea-baths. I will go this hour to Coslin for that purpose! but no, no, I cannot travel so rashly. Pollnitz, you must find me a courier."

"I will try," said Pollnitz. "One can buy all the glories of this world for gold; and, I think, your highness will not regard a few louis d'or, more or less."

"Find me a messenger, and I will pay every hour of his journey with a gold piece."

"I will send my own servant, in half an hour he shall be ready."

"God be thanked! it will then, be possible to save him. Let me write this letter at once, and hasten your messenger. Let him fly as if he had wings—as if the wild winds of heaven bore him onward. The sooner he brings me the answer of the duke, the greater shall be his reward. Oh, I will reward him as if I were a rich queen, and not a poor, forsaken, sorrowful princess."

"Write, princess, write," cried Pollnitz, eagerly: "but not have the goodness to give me the hundred louis d'or before Mademoiselle Marwitz returns. I promised them to Weingarten for his news; you can add to them the ducats you were graciously pleased to bestow upon me."

Amelia did not reply; she stepped to the table and wrote a few lines, which she handed to Pollnitz.

"Take this," said she, almost contemptuously; "it is a draft upon my banker, Orguelin. I thank you for allowing your services to be paid for; it relieves me from all call to gratitude. Serve me faithfully in future, and you shall ever find my hand open and my purse full. And now give me time to write to the duke, and—"

"Princess, I hear Mademoiselle Marwitz returning!"

Amelia left the writing-table hastily, and advanced to the door through which Mademoiselle Marwitz must enter.

"Ah, you are come at last," said she, as the door opened. "I was about to seek you. I feared you could not find the paper."

"It was very difficult to find amongst such a mass of letters and papers," said Mademoiselle Marwitz, whose suspicious glance was now wandering round the room. "I succeeded, however, at last; here is the manuscript, your highness."

The princess took it and examined it carefully. "Ah, I thought so," she said. "A monologue which Voltaire wrote for me, is missing. I gave it to the king, and I sec he has not returned it. I think my memory is the only faculty which retains its power. It is my misfortune that I cannot forget! I will test it to-day and try to write this monologue from memory. I must be alone, however. I pray you, mademoiselle, to go into the saloon with Pollnitz; he can entertain you with the Chronique Scandaleuse of our most virtuous court, while I am writing.—And now," said she, when she found herself alone, "may God give me power to reach the heart of the duke, and win him to my purpose!"

With a firm hand she wrote:

"Because you are happy, duke, you will have pity for the wretched. For a few days past, you have had your young and lovely wife at your side, and experienced the pure bliss of a happy union; you will therefore comprehend the despair of those who love as fondly, and can never be united. And now, I would remind you of a day on which it was in my power to obtain for you a great favor from my brother the king. At that time you promised me to return this service tenfold, should it ever be in your power, and you made me promise, if I should ever need assistance, to turn to you alone! My hour has come! I need your help; not for myself! God and death alone can help me. I demand your aid for a man who is chained with me to the galleys. You know him—have mercy upon him! Perhaps he will arrive at your court in the same hour with my letter. Duke, will you be the jailer of the wretched and the powerless, who is imprisoned only because I am the daughter of a king? Are your officers constables? will you allow them to cast into an eternal prison him for whom I have wept night and day for many long years?"

"Oh, my God! My God! you have given wings to the birds of the air; you have given to the horse his fiery speed; you have declared that man is the king of creation; you have marked upon his brow the seal of freedom, and this is his holiest possession. Oh, friend, will you consent that a noble gentleman, who has nothing left but his freedom, shall be unjustly deprived of it! Duke, I call upon you! Be a providence for my unhappy friend, and set him at liberty. And through my whole life long I will bless and honor you! AMELIA."

"If he does not listen to this outcry of my soul," she whispered, as she folded and sealed the letter—"if he has the cruelty to let me plead in vain, then in my death-hour I will curse him, and charge him with being the murderer of my last hope!"

The princess called Pollnitz, and, with an expressive glance, she handed him the letter.

"Truly, my memory has not failed me," she said to Mademoiselle Marwitz, who entered behind Pollnitz, and whose sharp eyes were fixed upon the letter in the baron's hand. "I have been able to write the whole monologue. Give this paper to my brother, Pollnitz; I have added a few friendly lines, and excused myself for declining the invitation. I cannot see this drama."

"Well, it seems to me I have made a lucrative affair of this," said Pollnitz to himself, as he left the princess. "I promised Weingarten only fifty louis d'or, so fifty remain over for myself, without counting the ducats which the princess intends for me. Besides, I shall be no such fool as to give my servant, who steals from me every day, the reward the princess has set apart for him; and if I give him outside work to do, it is my opportunity; he is my slave, and the reward is properly mine."

"Listen, John!" Said Pollnitz to his servant, as he entered his apartment. Poor John was, at the same time, body-servant, jockey, and coachman. "Listen; do you know exactly how much you have loaned me?"

"To a copper, your excellency," said John, joyfully. Poor John thought that the hour of settlement had come. "Your excellency owes me fifty-three thalers, four groschen, and five pennies."

"Common soul," cried Pollnitz, shrugging his shoulders contemptuously, "to be able to keep in remembrance such pitiful things as groschen and coppers. Well, I have a most pressing and important commission for you. You must saddle your horse immediately, and hasten to deliver this letter to the Duke of Wurtemberg. You must ride night and day and not rest till you arrive and deliver this packet into the duke's own hands. I will then allow you a day's rest for yourself and horse; your return must be equally rapid. If you are here again in eight days, I will reward you royally."

"That is to say, your excellency—" said John, in breathless expectation.

"That is to say, I will pay you half the sum I owe you, if you are here in eight days; if you are absent longer, you will get only a third."

"And if I return a day earlier?" Said John, sighing.

"I will give you a few extra thalers as a reward," said Pollnitz.

"But your excellency will, besides this, give me money for the journey," said John, timidly.

"Miserable, shameless beggar!" Cried Pollnitz; "always demanding more than one is willing to accord you. Learn from your noble master that there is nothing more pitiful, more sordid than gold, and that those only are truly noble, who serve others for honor's sake, and give no thought to reward."

"But, your grace, I have already the honor to have lent you all my money. I have not even a groschen to buy food for myself and horse on our journey."

"As for your money, sir, it is, under all circumstances, much safer with me than with you. You would surely spend it foolishly, while I will keep it together. Besides this, there is no other way to make servants faithful and submissive but to bind them to you by the miserable bond of selfishness. You would have left me a hundred times, if you had not been tied down by your own pitiful interests. You know well that if you leave me without my permission, the law allows me to punish you, by giving the money I owe you to the poor. But enough of foolish talking! Make ready for the journey; in half an hour you must leave Berlin behind you. I will give you a few thalers to buy food. Now, hasten! Remember, if you remain away longer than eight days, I will give you only a third of the money I am keeping for you."

This terrible threat had its effect upon poor John.

In eight days Pollnitz sought the princess, and with a triumphant glance, slipped a letter into her hand, which read thus:

"I thank you, princess, that you have remembered me, and given me an opportunity to aid the unhappy. You are right. God made man to be free. I am no jailer, and my officers are not constables. They have, indeed, the duty to conduct the unhappy man who has been for three days the guest of my house, farther on toward the fortress, but his feet and his hands shall be free, and if he takes a lesson from the bird in velocity, and from the wild horse in speed, his present escape will cost him less than his flight from Glatz. My officers cannot be always on the watch, and God's world is large; it is impossible to guard every point. My soldiers accompany him to the brook Coslin. I commend the officer who will be discharged for neglect of duty to your highness. FERDINAND."

"He will have my help and my eternal gratitude," whispered Amelia; she then pressed the letter of the duke passionately to her lips. "Oh, my God! I feel to-day what I have never before thought possible, that one can be happy without happiness. If fate will be merciful, and not thwart the noble purpose of Duke Ferdinand, from this time onward I will never murmur—never complain. I will demand nothing of the future; never more to see him, never more to hear from him, only that he may be free and happy."

In the joy of her heart she not only fulfilled her promise to give the messenger a gold piece for every hour of his journey, but she added a costly diamond pin for Pollnitz, which the experienced baron, even while receiving it from the trembling hand of the princess, valued at fifty louis d'or.

The baron returned with a well-filled purse and a diamond pin to his dwelling, and with imposing solemnity he called John into his boudoir.

"John," said he, "I am content with you. You have promptly fulfilled my commands. You returned the seventh day, and have earned the extra thalers. As for your money, how much do I owe you?"

"Fifty-three thalers, four groschen, and five pennies."

"And the half of this is—"

"Twenty-seven thalers, fourteen groschen, two and a half pennies," said John, with a loudly beating heart and an expectant smile. He saw that the purse was well filled, and that his master was taking out the gold pieces.

"I will give you, including your extra guldens, twenty-eight thalers, fourteen groschen, two and a half pennies." said Pollnitz, laying some gold pieces on the table. "Here are six louis d'or, or thirty-six thalers in gold to reckon up; the fractions you claim are beneath my dignity. Take them, John, they are yours."

John uttered a cry of rapture, and sprang forward with outstretched hands to seize his gold. He had succeeded in gathering up three louis d'or, when the powerful hand of the baron seized him and held him back.

"John," said he, "I read in your wild, disordered countenance that you are a spendthrift, and this gold, which you have earned honestly, will soon be wasted in boundless follies. It is my duty, as your conscientious master and friend, to prevent this. I cannot allow you to take all of this money—only one-half; only three louis d'or. I will put the other three with the sum which I still hold, and take care of it for you."

With an appearance of firm principle and piety, he grasped the three louis d'or upon which the sighing John fixed his tearful eyes.

"And now, what is the amount," said Pollnitz, gravely, "which you have placed in my hands for safe-keeping?"

"Thirty-two thalers, fourteen groschen, and five pennies," said John; "and then the fractions from the three louis d'ors makes a thaler and eight groschen."

"Pitiful miser! You dare to reckon fractions against your master, who, in his magnanimity, has just presented, you with gold! This is a meanness which merits exemplary punishment."

CHAPTER II
TRENCK ON HIS WAY TO PRISON

Before the palace of the Duke of Wurtemberg, in Coslin, stood the light, open carriage in which the duke was accustomed to make excursions, when inclined to carry the reins himself, and enjoy freedom and the pure, fresh air, without etiquette and ceremony.

To-day, however, the carriage was not intended for an ordinary excursion, but to transport a prisoner. This prisoner was no other than the unhappy Frederick Trenck, whom the cowardly republic of Dantzic, terrified at the menaces of the king, had delivered up to the Prussian police.

The intelligence of his unhappy fate flew like a herald before him. He was guarded by twelve hussars, and the sad procession was received everywhere throughout the journey with kindly sympathy. All exerted themselves to give undoubted proofs of pity and consideration. Even the officers in command, who sat by him in the carriage, and who were changed at every station, treated him as a loved comrade in arms, and not as a state prisoner.

But while all sighed and trembled for him, Trenck alone was gay; his countenance alone was calm and courageous. Not one moment, during the three days he passed in the palace of the duke, was his youthful and handsome face clouded by a single shadow. Not one moment did that happy, cheerful manner, by which he won all hearts, desert him. At the table, he was the brightest and wittiest; his amusing narratives, anecdotes, and droll ideas made not only the duke, but the duchess and her maids, laugh merrily. In the afternoons, in the saloon of the duchess, he astonished and enraptured the whole court circle by improvising upon any given theme, and by the tasteful and artistic manner in which he sang the national ballads he had learned on his journeys through Italy, Germany, and Russia. At other times, he conversed with the duke upon philosophy and state policy; and he was amazed at the varied information and wisdom of this young man, who seemed an experienced soldier and an adroit diplomat, a profound statesman, and a learned historian. By his dazzling talents, he not only interested but enchained his listeners.

The duke felt sadly that it was not possible to retain the prisoner longer in Coslin. Three days of rest was the utmost that could be granted Trenck, without exciting suspicion. He sighed, as he told Trenck that his duty required of him to send him further on his dark journey.

Trenck received this announcement with perfect composure, with calm self-possession. He took leave of the duke and duchess, and thanked them gayly for their gracious reception.

"I hope that my imprisonment will be of short duration, and then your highness will, I trust, allow me to return to you, and offer the thanks of a free man."

"May we soon meet again!" said the duke, and he looked searchingly upon Trenck, as if he wished to read his innermost thoughts. "As soon as you are free, come to me. I will not forsake you, no matter under what circumstances you obtain your freedom."

Had Trenck observed the last emphatic words of the duke, and did he understand their meaning? The duke did not know. No wink of the eyelid, not the slightest sign, gave evidence that Trenck had noticed their significance. He bowed smilingly, left the room with a firm step, and entered the carriage.

The duke called back the ordnance officer who was to conduct him to the next station.

"You have not forgotten my command?" said he.

"No, your highness, I have not forgotten; and obedience is a joyful duty, which I will perform punctually."

"You will repeat this command, in my name, to the officer at the next station, and commission him to have it repeated at every station where my regiments are quartered. Every one shall give Trenck an opportunity to escape, but silently; no word must be spoken to him on the subject. It must depend upon him to make use of the most favorable moment. My intentions toward him must be understood by him without explanations. He who is so unfortunate as to allow the prisoner to escape, can only be blamed for carelessness in duty. Upon me alone will rest the responsibility to the King of Prussia. You shall proceed but five or six miles each day; at this rate of travel it will take four days to reach the last barracks of my soldiers, and almost the entire journey lies through dark, thick woods, and solitary highways. Now go, and may God be with you!"

The duke stepped to the window to see Trenck depart, and to give him a last greeting.

"Well, if he is not at liberty in the next few days, it will surely not be my fault," murmured Duke Ferdinand, "and Princess Amelia cannot reproach me."

As Trenck drove from the gate, Duke Ferdinand turned thoughtfully away. He was, against his will, oppressed by sad presentiments. For Trenck, this journey over the highways in the light, open carriage, was actual enjoyment. He inhaled joyfully the pure, warm, summer air—his eyes rested with rapture upon the waving corn-fields, and the blooming, fragrant meadows through which they passed. With gay shouts and songs he seemed to rival the lark as she winged her way into the clouds above him. He was innocent, careless, and happy as a child. The world of Nature had been shut out from him in the dark, close carriage which had brought him to Coslin; she greeted him now with glad smiles and gay adorning. It seemed as if she were decorated for him with her most odorous blossoms and most glorious sunshine—as if she sent her softest breeze to kiss his cheek and whisper love—greetings in his ear. With upturned, dreamy glance, he followed the graceful movements of the pure, white clouds, and the rapid flight of the birds. Trenck was so happy in even this appearance of freedom, that he mistook it for liberty.

The carriage rolled slowly over the sandy highways, and now entered a wood. The sweet odor of the fir-trees drew from Trenck a cry of rapture. He had felt the heat of the sun to be oppressive, and he now laid his head back under the shadow of the thick trees with a feeling of gladness.

"It will take us some hours to get through this forest," said the ordnance officer, "It is one of the thickest woods in this region, and the terror of the police. The escaped prisoner who succeeds in concealing himself here, may defy discovery. It is impossible to pursue him in these dark, tangled woods, and a few hours conduct him to the sea-shore, where there are ever small fishing-boats ready to receive the fugitive and place him safely upon some passing ship. But excuse me, sir! the sun has been blazing down so hotly upon my head that I feel thoroughly wearied, and will follow the example of my coachman. Look! he is fast asleep, and the horses are moving on of their own good-will. Good-night, Baron Trenck."

He closed his eyes, and in a short time his loud snores and the nodding of his head from side to side gave assurance that he, also, was locked in slumber.

Profound stillness reigned around. Trenck gave himself wholly to the enjoyment of the moment. The peaceful stillness of the forest, interrupted only at intervals by the snorting of the horses, the sleepy chatter of the birds among the dark green branches, and the soft rustling and whispering of the trees, filled him with delight.

"It is clear," he said to himself, "that this arrest in Dantzic was only a manoeuvre to terrify me. I rejected the proposal of the Prussian ambassador in Vienna, to return to Berlin and enter again the Prussian service, so the king wishes to punish and frighten me. This is a jest—a comedy!—which the king is carrying on at my expense. If I were really regarded as a deserter, as a prisoner for the crime of high treason, no officer would dare to guard me so carelessly. In the beginning, I was harshly treated, in order to alarm and deceive me, and truly those twelve silent hussars, continually surrounding the closed carriage, had rather a melancholy aspect, and I confess I was imposed upon. But the mask has fallen, and I see behind the smiling, good-humored face of the king. He loved me truly once, and was as kind as a father. The old love has awakened and spoken in my favor. Frederick wishes to have me again in Berlin—that is all; and he knows well that I can be of service to him. He who has his spies everywhere, knows that no one else can give him such definite information as to the intentions and plans of Russia as I can—that no one knows so certainly what the preparations for war, now going on throughout the whole of Russia, signify. Yes, yes: so it is! Frederick will have me again in his service; he knows of my intimacy with the all-powerful wife of Bestuchef; that I am in constant correspondence with her, and in this way informed of all the plans of the Russian government. [Footnote: Frederick Trenck's "Memoirs."] Possibly, the king intends to send me as a secret ambassador to St. Petersburg! That would, indeed, open a career to me, and bring me exalted honor, and perhaps make that event possible which has heretofore only floated before my dazzled sight like a dream-picture. Oh, Amelia! noblest, most constant of women! could the dreams of our youth be realized? If fate, softened by your tears and your heroic courage, would at last unite you with him you have so fondly and so truly loved! Misled by youth, presumption, and levity, I have sometimes trifled with my most holy remembrances, sometimes seemed unfaithful; but my love to you has never failed; I have worn it as a talisman about my heart. I have ever worshipped you, I have ever hoped in you, and I will believe in you always, if I doubt and despair of all others. Oh, Amelia! protecting angel of my life! perhaps I may now return to you. I shall see you again, look once more into your beauteous eyes, kneel humbly before you, and receive absolution for my sins. They were but sins of the flesh, my soul had no part in them. I will return to you, and live free, honored, and happy by your side. I know this by the gracious reception of the duke; I know it by the careless manner in which I am guarded. Before the officer went to sleep he told me how securely a fugitive could hide himself in these woods. I, however, have no necessity to hide myself; no misfortune hovers over me, honor and gladness beckon me on. I will not be so foolish as to fly; life opens to me new and flowery paths, greets me with laughing hopes." *[Footnote: "Frederick Trenck's Memoirs."]*

Wholly occupied with these thoughts, Trenck leaned back in the carriage and gave himself up to bright dreams of the future. Slowly the horses moved through the deep, white sand, which made the roll of the wheels noiseless, and effaced instantaneously the footprints of men. The officer still slept, the coachman had dropped the reins, and nodded here and there as if intoxicated. The wood was drear and empty; no human dwelling, no human face was seen. Had Trenck wished to escape, one spring from the low, open carriage; a hundred hasty steps would have brought him to a thicket where discovery was impossible; the carriage would have rolled on quietly, and when the sleepers aroused themselves, they would have had no idea of the direction Trenck had taken. The loose and rolling sand would not have retained his footprints, and the whispering trees would not have betrayed him.

Trenck would not fly; he was full of romance, faith, and hope; his sanguine temper painted his future in enchanting colors. No, he would not flee, he had faith in his star. Life's earnest tragedy had yet for him a smiling face, and life's bitter truths seemed alluring visions. No, the king only wished to try him; he wished to see if he could frighten him into an effort to escape; he gave him the opportunity for flight, but if he made use of it, he would be lost forever in the eyes of Frederick, and his prospects utterly destroyed. If he bravely suffered the chance of escape to pass by, and arrived in Berlin, to all appearance a prisoner, the king would have the agreeable task of undeceiving him, and Trenck would have shown conclusively that he had faith in the king's magnanimity, and gave himself up to him without fear. He would have proved also that his conscience was clear, and that, without flattering, he could yield himself to the judgment of the king. No, Trenck would not fly. In Berlin, liberty, love, and Amelia awaited him; he would lose all this by flight; it would all remain his if he did not allow himself to be enticed by the flattering goddess, opportunity, who now beckoned and nodded smilingly from behind every tree and every thicket. Trenck withstood these enticements during three long days; with careless indifference he passed slowly on through this lonely region; in his arrogant blindness and self-confidence he did not observe the careworn and anxious looks of the officers who conducted him; he did not hear or understand the low, hesitating insinuations they dared to speak.

"This is your last resting-point," said the officer who had conducted him from the last station. "You will remain here this afternoon, and early to-morrow morning the cavalry officer Von Halber will conduct you to Berlin, where the last barracks of our regiment are to be found; from that point the infantry garrison will take charge of your further transportation."

"I shall not make their duties difficult," said Trenck, gayly. "You see I am a good-natured prisoner; no Argus eyes are necessary, as I have no intention to flee."

The officer gazed into his calm, smiling face with amazement, and then stepped out with the officer Von Halber, into whose house they had now entered, to make known his doubts and apprehensions.

"Perhaps the opportunities which have been offered him have not been sufficiently manifest," said Von Halber. "Perhaps he has not regarded them as safe, and he fears a failure. In that he is right; a vain attempt at flight would be much more prejudicial to him than to yield himself without opposition. Well, I will see that he has now a sure chance to escape, and you may believe he will be cunning enough to take advantage of it. You may say this much to his highness the duke."

"But do not forget that the duke commanded us not to betray his intention to prepare these opportunities by a single word. This course would compromise the duke and all of us."

"I understand perfectly," said Von Halber; "I will speak eloquently by deeds, and not with words."

True to this intention, Von Halber, after having partaken of a gay dinner with Trenck and several officers, left his house, accompanied by all his servants.

"The horses must be exercised," said he; and, as he was unmarried, no one remained in the house but Trenck.

"You will be my house-guard for several hours," said the officer to Trenck, who was standing at the door as he drove off. "I hope no one will come to disturb your solitude. My officers all accompany me, and I have no acquaintance in this little village. You will be entirely alone, and if, on my return, I find that you have disappeared in mist and fog, I shall believe that ennui has extinguished you—reduced you to a bodiless nothing."

"Well, I think he must have understood that," said Von Halber, as he dashed down the street, followed by his staff. "He must be blind and deaf if he does not flee from the fate before him."

Trenck, alas, had not understood. He believed in no danger, and did not, therefore, see the necessity for flight. He found this quiet, lonely house inexpressibly wearisome. He wandered through the rooms, seeking some object of interest, or some book which would enable him to pass the tedious hours. The cavalry officer was a gallant and experienced soldier, but he was no scholar, and had nothing to do with books. Trenck's search was in vain. Discontented and restless, he wandered about, and at last entered the little court which led to the stable. A welcome sound fell on his ears, and made his heart beat joyfully; with rapid steps he entered the stable. Two splendid horses stood in the stalls, snorting and stamping impatiently; they were evidently riding-horses, for near them hung saddles and bridles. Their nostrils dilated proudly as they threw their heads back to breathe the fresh air which rushed in at the open door. It appeared to Trenck that their flashing eyes were pleading to him for liberty and action.

"Poor beasts," said he, stepping forward, and patting and caressing them—"poor beasts, you also pine for liberty, and hope for my assistance; but I cannot, I dare not aid you. Like you, I also am a prisoner, and like you also, a prisoner to my will. If you would use your strength, one movement of your powerful muscles would tear your bonds asunder, and your feet would bear you swiftly like wings through the air. If I would use the present opportunity, which beckons and smiles upon me, it would be only necessary to spring upon your back and dash off into God's fair and lovely world. We would reach our goal, we would be free, but we would both be lost; we would be recaptured, and would bitterly repent our short dream of self-acquired freedom. It is better for us both that we remain as we are; bound, not with chains laid upon our bodies, but by wisdom and discretion."

So saying, he smoothed tenderly the glossy throat of the gallant steed, whose joyful neigh filled his heart with an inexplicable melancholy.

"I must leave you," murmured he, shudderingly; "your lusty neighing intoxicates my senses, and reminds me of green fields and fragrant meadows; of the broad highways, and the glad feeling of liberty which one enjoys when flying through the world on the back of a gallant steed. No! No! I dare no longer look upon you; all my wisdom and discretion might melt away, and I might be allured to seek for myself that freedom which I must receive alone at the hands of the king, in Berlin."

With hasty steps Trenck left the stable and returned to the house, where he stretched himself upon the sofa, and gave himself up to dreamland. It was twilight when Halber returned from his long ride.

"All is quiet and peaceful," said he, as he entered the house. "The bird has flown, this time; he found the opportunity favorable."

With a contented smile, he entered his room, but his expression changed suddenly, and his trembling lips muttered a soldier's curse. There lay Trenck in peaceful slumber; his handsome, youthful face was bright and free from care, and those must be sweet dreams which floated around him, for he smiled in his sleep.

"Poor fellow!" said Von Halber, shaking his head; "he must be mad, or struck with blindness, and cannot see the yawning abyss at his feet." He awakened Trenck, and asked him how he had amused himself, during the long hours of solitude.

"I looked through all your house, and then entered the stables and gladdened my heart by the sight of your beautiful horses."

"Thunder and lightning! You have then seen my horses," cried Halber, thoroughly provoked. "Did no wish arise in your heart to mount one and seek your liberty?"

Frederick Trenck smiled. "The wish, indeed, arose in my heart, but I suppressed it manfully. Do you not see, dear Halber, that it would be unthankful and unknightly to reward in this cowardly and contemptible way the magnanimous confidence you have shown me."

"Truly, you are an honorable gentleman," cried Halber, greatly touched; "I had not thought of that. It would not have been well to flee from my house."

"To-morrow he will fly," thought the good-natured soldier, "when once more alone—to-morrow, and the opportunity shall not be wanting."

Von Halber left his house early in the morning to conduct his prisoner to Berlin. No one accompanied them; no one but the coachman, who sat upon the box and never looked behind him.

Their path led through a thick wood. Von Halber entertained the prisoner as the lieutenant had done who conducted Trenck the day he left Coslin. He called his attention to the denseness of the forest, and spoke of the many fugitives who had concealed themselves there till pursuit was abandoned. He then invited Trenck to get down and walk with him, near the carriage.

As Trenck accepted the invitation, and strolled along by his side in careless indifference, Von Halber suddenly observed that the ground was covered with mushrooms.

"Let us gather a few," said he; "the young wife of one of my friends understands how to make a glorious dish of them, and if I take her a large collection, she will consider it a kind attention. Let us take our hats and handkerchiefs, and fill them. You will take the right path into the wood, and I the left. In one hour we will meet here again."

Without waiting for an answer, the good Halber turned to the left in the wood, and was lost in the thicket. In an hour he returned to the carriage, and found Trenck smilingly awaiting him.

He turned pale, and with an expression of exasperation, he exclaimed:

"You have not then lost yourself in the woods?"

"I have not lost myself," said Trenck, quietly; "and I have gathered a quantity of beautiful mushrooms."

Trenck handed him his handkerchief, filled with small, round mushrooms. Halber threw them with a sort of despair into the carriage, and then, without saying one word, he mounted and nodded to Trenck to follow him.

"And now let us be off," said he, shortly. "Coachman, drive on!"

He leaned back in the carriage, and with frowning brow he gazed up into the heavens.

Slowly the carriage rolled through the sand, and it seemed as if the panting, creeping horses shrank back from reaching their goal, the boundary-line of the Wurtembergian dragoons. Trenck had followed his companion's example, and leaned back in the carriage. Halber was gloomy and filled with dark forebodings. Trenck was gay and unembarrassed; not the slightest trace of care or mistrust could be read in his features.

They moved onward silently. The air was fresh and pure, the heavens clear; but a dark cloud was round about the path of this dazzled, blinded young officer. The birds sang of it on the green boughs, hut Trenck would not understand them. They sang of liberty and gladness; they called to him to follow their example, and fly far from the haunts of men! The dark wood echoed Fly! fly! in powerful organ-tones, but Trenck took them for the holy hymns of God's peaceful, sleeping world. He heard not the trees, as with warning voices they bowed down and murmured, Flee! flee! Come under our shadow, we will conceal you till the danger be overpast' Flee! flee! Misfortune, like a cruel vulture, is floating over you—already her fangs are extended to grasp you. The desert winds, in wild haste rushed by and covering this poor child of sorrow with clouds of dust, whispered in his ear, Fly! fly!—follow my example and rush madly backward! Misfortune advances to meet you, and a river of tears flows down the path you are blindly following. Turn your head and flee, before this broad, deep stream overtakes you. The creaking wheels seemed to sob out. Fly! fly! we are rolling you onward to a dark and eternal prison! Do you not hear the clashing of chains? Do you not see the open grave at your feet? These are your chains!—that is your grave, already prepared for the living, glowing heart! Fly! then, fly! You are yet free to choose. The clouds which swayed on over the heavens, traced in purple and gold the warning words, Fly! fly! or you look upon us for the last time! Upon the anxious face of Von Halber was also to be seen, Fly now, it is high time! I see the end of the wood!—I see the first houses of Boslin. Fly! then, fly!—it is high time! Alas, Trenck's eyes were blinded, and his ears were filled with dust.

"Those whom demons will destroy, they first strike with blindness." Trenck's evil genius had blinded his eyes—his destruction was sure. There remained no hope of escape. The carriage had reached the end of the wood and rolled now over the chausse to Boslin.

But what means this great crowd before the stately house which is decorated with the Prussian arms? What means this troop of soldiers who with stern, frowning brows, surround the dark coach with the closed windows?

"We are in Boslin," said Von Halber, pointing toward the group of soldiers. "That is the post-house, and, as you see, we are expected."

For the first time Trenck was pale, and horror was written in his face. "I am lost!" stammered he, completely overcome, and sinking back into the carriage he cast a wild, despairing glance around him, and seized the arm of Halber with a powerful hand.

"Be merciful, sir! oh, be merciful! Let us move more slowly. Turn back, oh, turn back! just to the entrance of the wood—only to the entrance of the street!"

"You see that is impossible," said Von Halber, sadly. "We are recognized; if we turn back now, they will welcome us with bullets."

"It were far better for me to die," murmured Trenck, "than to enter that dark prison—that open grave!"

"Alas! you would not fly—you would not understand me. I gave you many opportunities, but you would not avail yourself of them."

"I was mad, mad!" cried Trenck. "I had confidence in myself—I had faith in my good star—but the curse of my evil genius has overtaken me. Oh, my God! I am lost, lost! All my hopes were deceptive—the king is my irreconcilable enemy, and he will revenge my past life on my future! I have this knowledge too late. Oh, Halber! go slowly, slowly; I must give you my last testament. Mark well what I say—these are the last words of a man who is more to be pitied than the dying. It is a small service which I ask of you, but my existence depends upon it: Go quickly to the Duke of Wurtemberg and say this to him: 'Frederick von Trenck sends Duke Ferdinand his last greeting! He is a prisoner, and in death's extremity. Will the duke take pity on him, and convey this news to her whom he knows to be Trenck's friend? Tell her Trenck is a prisoner, and hopes only in her!' Will you swear to me to do this?"

"I swear it," said Von Halber, deeply moved.

The carriage stopped. Von Halber sprang down and greeted the officer who was to take charge of Trenck. The soldiers placed themselves on both sides of the coach, and the door was opened. Trenck cast a last despairing, imploring glance to heaven, then, with a firm step, approached the open coach. In the act of entering, he turned once more to the officer Von Halber, whose friendly eyes were darkened with tears.

"You will not forget, sir!"

These simply, sadly-spoken words, breaking the solemn, imposing silence, made an impression upon the hearts of even the stern soldiers around them.

"I will not forget," said Von Halber, solemnly.

Trenck bowed and entered the coach. The officer followed him and closed the door. Slowly, like a funeral procession, the coach moved on. Von Halber gazed after him sadly.

"He is right, he is more to be pitied than the dying. I will hasten to fulfil his last testament."

Eight days later, the Princess Amelia received through the hands of Pollnitz a letter from Duke Ferdinand. As she read it, she uttered a cry of anguish, and sank insensible upon the floor. The duke's letter contained these words:

"All my efforts were in vain; he would not fly, would not believe in his danger. In the casemates of Magdeburg sits a poor prisoner, whose last words directed to me were these: 'Say to her whom you know that I am a prisoner, and hope only in her.'"

CHAPTER III
PRINCE HENRY AND HIS WIFE

Prince Henry walked restlessly backward and forward in his study; his brow was stern, and a strange fire flamed in his eye. He felt greatly agitated and oppressed, and scarcely knew the cause himself. Nothing had happened to disturb his equanimity and give occasion for his wayward mood. The outside world wore its accustomed gay and festal aspect. To-day, as indeed almost every day since the prince resided at Rheinsberg, preparations were being made for a gay entertainment. A country fete was to be given in the woods near the palace, and all the guests were to appear as shepherds and shepherdesses.

Prince Henry had withdrawn to his own room to assume the tasteful costume which had been prepared for him; but he seemed to have entirely forgotten his purpose. The tailor and the friseur awaited him in vain in his dressing-room; he forgot their existence. He paced his room with rapid steps, and his tightly-compressed lips opened from time to time to utter a few broken, disconnected words.

Of what was the prince thinking? He did not know, or he would not confess it to himself. Perhaps he dared not look down deep into his heart and comprehend the new feelings and new wishes which were struggling there.

At times he stood still, and looked with a wild, rapt expression into the heavens, as if they alone could answer the mysterious questions his soul was whispering to him; then passed on with his hand pressed on his brow to control or restrain the thoughts which agitated him. He did not hear a light tap upon the door, he did not see it open, and his most intimate and dearest friend, Count Kalkreuth enter, dressed in the full costume of a shepherd.

Count Kalkreuth stood still, and did nothing to call the attention of the prince to his presence. He remained at the door; his face was also dark and troubled, and the glance which he fixed upon Prince Henry was almost one of hatred.

The prince turned, and the count's expression changed instantly; he stepped gayly forward and said:

"Your royal highness sees my astonishment at finding you lost in such deep thought, and your toilet not even commenced. I stand like Lot's blessed wife, turned to stone upon your threshold! Have you forgotten, my prince, that you commanded us all to be ready punctually at four o'clock? The castle clock is at this moment striking four. The ladies and gentlemen will now assemble in the music-saloon, as you directed, and you, prince, are not yet in costume."

"It is true," said Prince Henry, somewhat embarrassed, "I had forgotten; but I will hasten to make good my fault."

He stepped slowly, and with head bowed down, toward his dressing-room; at the door, he stood and looked back at the count.

"You are already in costume, my friend," said he, noticing for the first time the fantastic dress of the count. "Truly, this style becomes you marvellously; your bright-colored satin jacket shows your fine proportions as advantageously as your captain's uniform. But what means this scarf which you wear upon your shoulder?"

"These are the colors of my shepherdess," said the count, with a constrained smile.

"Who is your shepherdess?"

"Your highness asks that, when you yourself selected her!" said Kalkreuth, astonished.

"Yes it is true; I forgot," said the prince. "The princess, my wife, is your shepherdess. Well, I sincerely hope you may find her highness more gay and gracious than she was to me this morning, and that you may see the rare beauty of this fair rose, of which I only feel the thorns!"

While the prince was speaking, the count became deathly pale, and looked at him with painful distrust.

"It is true," he replied, "the princess is cold and reserved toward her husband. Without doubt, this is the result of a determination to meet your wishes fully, and to remain clearly within the boundary which your highness at the time of your marriage, more than a year ago, plainly marked out for her. The princess knows, perhaps too well, that her husband is wholly indifferent to her beauty and her expression, and therefore feels herself at liberty to yield to each changeful mood without ceremony in your presence."

"You are right," said Prince Henry, sadly, "she is wholly indifferent to me, and I have told her so. We will speak no more of it. What, indeed, are the moods of the princess to me? I will dress, go to the music-saloon, and ask for forgiveness in my name for my delay. I will soon be ready; I will seek the princess in her apartments, and we will join you in a few moments."

The prince bowed and left the room. Kalkreuth gazed after him thoughtfully and anxious.

"His manner is unaccountably strange to-day," whispered he. "Has he, perhaps, any suspicion; and these apparently artless questions and remarks this distraction and forgetfulness—But no, no! it is impossible, he can know nothing—no one has betrayed me. It is the anguish of my conscience which makes me fearful; this suffering I must bear, it is the penalty I pay for my great happiness." The count sighed deeply and withdrew.

The prince completed his toilet, and sought the princess in her apartment, in the other wing of the castle. With hasty steps he passed through the corridors; his countenance was anxious and expectant, his eyes were glowing and impatient, haste marked every movement; he held in his hand a costly bouquet of white camelias. When he reached the anteroom of the princess he became pallid, and leaned for a moment, trembling and gasping for breath, against the wall; he soon, however, by a strong effort, controlled himself, entered, and commanded the servant to announce him.

The Princess Wilhelmina received her husband with a stiff, ceremonious courtesy, which, in its courtly etiquette, did not correspond with the costume she had assumed. The proud and stately princess was transformed into an enchanting, lovely shepherdess. It was, indeed, difficult to decide if the princess were more beautiful in her splendid court toilet, adorned with diamonds, and wearing on her high, clear brow a sparkling diadem, proud and conscious of her beauty and her triumphs; or now, in this artistic costume, in which she was less imposing, but more enchanting and more gracious.

Wilhelmina wore an under-skirt of white satin, a red tunic, gayly embroidered and festooned with white roses; a white satin bodice, embroidered with silver, defined her full but pliant form, and displayed her luxurious bust in its rare proportions; a bouquet of red roses was fastened upon each shoulder, and held the silvery veil which half concealed the lovely throat and bosom. The long, black, unpowdered hair fell in graceful ringlets about her fair neck, and formed a dark frame for the beautiful face, glowing with health, youth, and intellect. In her hair she wore a wreath of red and white roses, and a bouquet of the same in her bosom.

She was, indeed, dazzling in her beauty, and was, perhaps, conscious of her power; her eyes sparkled, and a ravishing smile played upon her lips as she looked up at the prince, who stood dumb and embarrassed before her, and could find no words to express his admiration.

"If it is agreeable to your highness, let us join your company," said the princess, at last, anxious to put an end to this interview. She extended her hand coolly to her husband; he grasped it, and held it fast, but still stood silently looking upon her.

"Madame," said he, at last, in low and hesitating tones—"madame, I have a request to make of you."

"Command me, my husband," said she, coldly; "what shall I do?"

"I do not wish to command, but to entreat," said the prince.

"Well, then, Prince Henry, speak your request."

The prince gave the bouquet of white camelias to his wife, and said, in a faltering, pleading voice, "I beg you to accept this bouquet from me, and to wear it to-day in your bosom, although it is not your shepherd who offers it!"

"No, not my shepherd, but my husband," said the princess, removing angrily the bouquet of roses from her bodice. "I must, of course, wear the flowers he gives me."

Without giving one glance at the flowers, she fastened them in her bosom.

"If you will not look upon them for my sake," said the prince, earnestly, "I pray you, give them one glance for the flowers' sake. You will at least feel assured that no other shepherdess is adorned with such a bouquet."

"Yes," said Wilhelmina, "these are not white roses; indeed, they seem to be artificial flowers; their leaves are hard and thick like alabaster, and dazzlingly white like snow. What flowers are these, my prince?"

"They are camelias. I recently heard you speak of these rare flowers, which had just been imported to Europe. I hoped to please you by placing them in your hands."

"Certainly; but I did not know that these new exotics were blooming in our land."

"And they are not," said Prince Henry. "This bouquet comes from Schwetzingen; there, only, in Germany, in the celebrated green-houses of the Margravine of Baden can they be seen."

"How, then, did you get them?" said the princess, astonished.

"I sent a courier to Schwetzingen; the blossoms were wrapped in moist, green moss, and are so well preserved, that they look as fresh as when they were gathered six days since."

"And you sent for them for me?" said Wilhelmina.

"Did you not express a wish to see them?" replied the prince; and his glance rested upon her with such ardent passion that, blushing, she cast her eyes to the ground, and stood still and ashamed before him.

"And you have not one little word of thanks?" said the prince, after a long pause. "Will you not fasten these pure flowers on your bosom, and allow them to die a happy death there? Alas! you are hard and cruel with me, princess; it seems to me that your husband dare claim from you more of kindliness and friendship."

"My husband!" cried she, in a mocking tone. She turned her eyes, searchingly, in every direction around the room. "It appears to me that we are alone and wholly unobserved, and that it is here unnecessary for us to play this comedy and call ourselves by those names which we adopted to deceive the world, and which you taught me to regard as empty titles. It is, indeed, possible that a wife should be more friendly and affectionate to her husband; but I do not believe that a lady dare give more encouragement to a cavalier than I manifest to your royal highness."

"You are more friendly to all the world than to me, Wilhelmina," said the prince, angrily. "You have a kindly word, a magic glance, a gracious reception for all others who approach you. To me alone are you cold and stern; your countenance darkens as soon as I draw near; the smile vanishes from your lips; your brow is clouded and your eyes are fixed upon me with almost an expression of contempt. I see, madame, that you hate me! Well, then, hate me; but I do not deserve your contempt, and I will not endure it! It is enough that you martyr me to death with your cutting coldness, your crushing indifference. The world, at least, should not know that you hate me, and I will not be publicly humiliated by you. What did I do this morning, for example? Why were you so cold and scornful? Wherefore did you check your gay laugh as I entered the room? wherefore did you refuse me the little flower you held in your hand, and then throw it carelessly upon the floor?"

The princess looked at him with flashing eyes.

"You ask many questions, sir, and on many points," said she, sharply. "I do not think it necessary to reply to them. Let us join our company." She bowed proudly and advanced, but the prince held her back.

"Do not go," said he, entreatingly, "do not go. Say first that you pardon me, that you are no longer angry. Oh, Wilhelmina, you do not know what I suffer; you can never know the anguish which tortures my soul."

"I know it well; on the day of our marriage your highness explained all. It was not necessary to return to this bitter subject. I have not forgotten one word spoken on that festive occasion."

"What do you mean, Wilhelmina? How could I, on our wedding-day, have made known to you the tortures which I now suffer, from which I was then wholly free, and in whose possibility I did not believe?"

"It is possible that your sufferings have become more intolerable," said the princess, coldly; "but you confided them to me fully and frankly at that time. It was, indeed, the only time since our marriage we had any thing to confide. Our only secret is that we do not love and never can love each other; that only in the eyes of the world are we married. There is no union of hearts."

"Oh, princess, your words are death!" And completely overcome, he sank upon a chair.

Wilhelmina looked at him coldly, without one trace of emotion.

"Death?" said she, "why should I slay you? We murder only those whom we love or hate. I neither love nor hate you."

"You are only, then, entirely indifferent to me," asked the prince.

"I think, your highness, this is what you asked of me, on our wedding-day. I have endeavored to meet your wishes, and thereby, at least, to prove to you that I had the virtue of obedience. Oh, I can never forget that hour," cried the princess. "I came a stranger, alone, ill from home-sickness and anguish of heart, to Berlin. I was betrothed according to the fate of princesses. I was not consulted! I did not know—I had never seen the man to whom I must swear eternal love and faith. This was also your sad fate, my prince. We had never met. We saw each other for the first time as we stood before God's altar, and exchanged our vows to the sound of merry wedding-bells, and the roar of cannon. I am always thinking that the bells ring and the cannon thunders at royal marriages, to drown the timid, trembling yes, forced from pallid, unwilling lips, which rings in the ears of God and men like a discord—like the snap of a harp-string. The bells chimed melodiously. No man heard the yes at which our poor hearts rebelled! We alone heard and understood! You were noble, prince; you had been forced to swear a falsehood before the altar; but in the evening, when we were alone in our apartment, you told me the frank and honest truth. State policy united us; we did not and could never love each other! You were amiable enough to ask me to be your friend—your sister; and to give me an immediate proof of a brother's confidence, you confessed to me that, with all the ardor and ecstasy of your youthful heart, you had loved a woman who betrayed you, and thus extinguished forever all power to love. I, my prince, could not follow your frank example, and give a like confidence. I had nothing to relate. I had not loved! I loved you not! I was therefore grateful when you asked no love from me. You only asked that, with calm indifference, we should remain side by side, and greet each other, before the world, with the empty titles of wife and husband. I accepted this proposal joyfully, to remain an object of absolute indifference to you, and to regard you in the same light. I cannot, therefore, comprehend why you now reproach me."

"Yes! yes! I said and did all that," said Prince Henry, pale and trembling with emotion. "I was a madman! More than that, I was a blasphemer! Love is as God—holy, invisible, and eternal; and he who does not believe in her immortality, her omnipresence, is like the heathen, who has faith only in his gods of wood and stone, and whose dull eyes cannot behold the invisible glory of the Godhead. My heart had at that time received its first wound, and because it bled and pained me fearfully, I believed it to be dead, and I covered it up with bitter and cruel remembrances, as in an iron coffin, from which all escape was impossible. An angel drew near, and laid her soft, fine hand upon my coffin, my wounds were healed, my youth revived, and I dared hope in happiness and a future. At first, I would not confess this to myself. At first, I thought to smother this new birth of my heart in the mourning veil of my past experience; but my heart was like a giant in his first manhood, and cast off all restraint; like Hercules in his cradle, he strangled the serpents which were hissing around him. It was indeed a painful happiness to know that I had again a heart, that I was capable of feeling the rapture and the pain, the longing, the hopes and fears, the enthusiasm and exaltation, the doubt and the despair which make the passion of love, and I have to thank you, Wilhelmina—you alone, you, my wife, for this new birth. You turn away your head, Wilhelmina! You smile derisively! It is true I have not the right to call you my wife. You are free to spurn me from you, to banish me forever into that cold, desert region to which I fled in the madness and blindness of my despair. But think well, princess; if you do this, you cast a shadow over my life. It is my whole future which I lay at your feet, a future for which fate perhaps intends great duties and greater deeds. I cannot fulfil these duties, I can perform no heroic deed, unless you, princess, grant me the blessing of happiness. I shall be a silent, unknown, and useless prince, the sad and pitiful hanger-on of a throne, despised and unloved, a burden only to my people, unless you give freedom and strength to my sick soul, which lies a prisoner at your feet. Wilhelmina, put an end to the tortures of the last few months, release me from the curse which binds my whole life in chains; speak but one word, and I shall have strength to govern the world, and prove to you that I am worthy of you. I will force the stars from heaven, and place them as a diadem upon your brow. Say only that you will try to love me, and I will thank you for happiness and fame."

Prince Henry was so filled with his passion and enthusiasm, that he did not remark the deadly pallor of Wilhelmina's face—that he did not see the look of anguish and horror with which her eyes rested for one moment upon him, then shrank blushingly and ashamed upon the floor. He seized her cold, nerveless hands, and pressed them to his heart; she submitted quietly. She seemed turned to stone.

"Be merciful, Wilhelmina; say that you forgive me—that you will try to love me."

The princess shuddered, and glanced up at him. "I must say that," murmured she, "and you have not once said that you love me."

The prince shouted with rapture, and, falling upon his knees, he exclaimed, "I love you! I adore you! I want nothing, will accept nothing, but you alone; you are my love, my hope, my future. Wilhelmina, if you do not intend me to die at your feet, say that you do not spurn me—open your arms and clasp me to your heart."

The princess stood immovable for a moment, trembling and swaying from side to side; her lips opened as if to utter a wild, mad cry—pain was written on every feature. The prince saw nothing of this—his lips were pressed upon her hand, and he did not look up—he did not see his wife press her pale lips tightly together to force back her cries of despair—he did not see that her eyes were raised in unspeakable agony to heaven.

The battle was over; the princess bowed over her husband, and her hands softly raised him from his knees. "Stand up, prince—I dare not see you lying at my feet. You have a right to my love—you are my husband."

Prince Henry clasped her closely, passionately in his arms.

CHAPTER IV
THE FETE IN THE WOODS

No fete was ever brighter and gayer than that of Rheinsberg. It is true, the courtly circle waited a long time before the beginning of their merry sports. Hours passed before the princely pair joined their guests in the music-saloon.

The sun of royalty came at last, shedding light and gladness. Never had the princess looked more beautiful—more rosy. She seemed, indeed, to blush at the consciousness of her own attractions. Never had Prince Henry appeared so happy, so triumphant, as to-day. His flashing eyes seemed to challenge the whole world to compete with his happiness; joy and hope danced in his eyes; never had he given so gracious, so kindly a greeting to every guest, as to-day.

The whole assembly was bright and animated and gave themselves up heartily to the beautiful idyl for which they had met together under the shadow of the noble trees in the fragrant woods of Rheinsberg. No gayer, lovelier shepherds and shepherdesses were ever seen in Arcadia, than those of Rheinsberg to-day. They laughed, and jested, and performed little comedies, and rejoiced in the innocent sports of the happy moment. Here wandered a shepherd and his shepherdess, chatting merrily; there, under the shadow of a mighty oak, lay a forlorn shepherd singing, accompanied by his zitter, a love-lorn ditty to his cruel shepherdess, who was leading two white lambs decked with ribbons, in a meadow near by, and replied to his tender pleading with mocking irony. Upon the little lake, in the neighborhood of which they had assembled, the snow-white swans swam majestically to and fro. The lovely shepherdesses stood upon the borders and enticed the swans around them, and laughed derisively at the shepherds who had embarked in the little boats, and were now driven sportively back in every direction, and could find no place to land.

Prince Henry loved this sort of fete, and often gave such at Rheinsberg, but never had he seemed to enjoy himself so thoroughly as to-day. His guests generally sympathized in his happiness, but there was one who looked upon his joyous face with bitterness. This was Louise du Trouffle, once Louise von Kleist, once the beloved of the prince.

She was married, and her handsome, amiable, and intelligent husband was ever by her side; but the old wounds still burned, and her pride bled at the contempt of the prince. She knew he was ignorant of the great sacrifice she had been forced to make—that he despised, in place of admiring and pitying her.

The prince, in order to show his utter indifference, had invited her husband and herself to court. In the pride of his sick and wounded heart, he resolved to convince the world that the beautiful Louise von Kleist had not scorned and rejected his love. In her presence he resolved to show his young wife the most lover-like attentions, and prove to his false mistress that he neither sought nor fled from her—that he had utterly forgotten her.

But Louise was not deceived by this acting. She understood him thoroughly, and knew better than the prince himself, that his indifference was assumed, and his contempt and scorn was a veil thrown over his betrayed and quivering heart to conceal his sufferings from her. Louise had the courage to accept Prince Henry's invitations, and to take part in all the festivities with which he ostentatiously celebrated his happiness. She had the courage to receive his cutting coldness, his cruel sarcasm, his contempt, with calm composure and sweet submission. With the smile of a stoic, she offered her defenceless breast to his poisoned arrows, and even the tortures she endured were precious in her sight. She was convinced that the prince had not relinquished or forgotten her—that his indifference and contempt was assumed to hide his living, breathing love. For some time past the change in the manners and bearing of the prince had not escaped the sharp, searching glance of the experienced coquette. For a long time he appeared not to see her—now she felt that he did not see her. He had been wont to say the most indifferent things to her in a fierce, excited tone—now he was self-possessed, and spoke to her softly and kindly.

"The wound has healed," said Louise du Trouffle to herself. "He no longer scorns because he no longer loves me." But she did not know that he had not only ceased to love her, but loved another passionately. This suspicion was excited, however, for the first time to-day. In the flashing eye, the glad smile, the proud glance which he fixed upon his fair young wife, Louise discovered that Henry had buried the old love and a new one had risen from its ashes. This knowledge tortured her heart in a wild storm of jealousy. She forgot all considerations of prudence, all fear, even of the king. She had been compelled to relinquish the hand of the prince, but she would not lose him wholly. Perhaps he would return to her when he knew what a fearful offering she had made to him. He would recognize her innocence, and mourn over the tortures he had inflicted during the last year. She would try this! She would play her last trump, and dare all with the hope of winning.

There stood the prince under the shadow of a large tree, gazing dreamily at his wife, who, with other shepherdesses, and her shepherd, Count Kalkreuth, was feeding the swans on the border of the lake. The prince was alone, and Louise rashly resolved to approach him. He greeted her with a slight nod, and turning his eyes again upon his wife, he said, carelessly, "Are you also here, Madame du Trouffle?"

"Your royal highness did me the honor to invite me—I am accustomed to obey your wishes, and I am here."

"That is kind," said the prince, abstractedly, still glancing at the princess.

Louise sighed deeply, and stepping nearer, she said, "Are you still angry with me, my prince? Have you never forgiven me?"

"What?" said the prince, quietly; "I do not remember that I have any thing to forgive."

"Ah, I see! you despise me still," said Louise, excitedly; "but I will bear this no longer! I will no longer creep about like a culprit, burdened with your curse and your scorn. You shall at least know what it cost me to earn your contempt—what a tearful sacrifice I was compelled to make to secure your supposed personal happiness. I gave up for you the happiness of my life, but I can and will no longer fill a place of shame in your memory. If, from time to time, your highness thinks of me, you shall do me justice!"

"I think no longer of you in anger," said the prince, smiling. "That sorrow has long since passed away."

"From your heart, prince, but not from mine! My heart bleeds, and will bleed eternally! You must not only forgive—you must do me justice. Listen, then: and so truly as there is a God above us, I will speak the truth. I did not betray you—I was not faithless. My heart and my soul I laid gladly at your feet, and thanked God for the fulness of my happiness. My thoughts, my existence, my future, was chained to you. I had no other will, no other wish, no other hope. I was your slave—I wanted nothing but your love."

"Ah, and then came this Monsieur du Trouffle, and broke your fetters—gave your heart liberty and wings for a new flight," said Prince Henry.

"No, then came the king and commanded me to give you up," murmured Louise; "then came the king, and forced me to offer up myself and my great love to your future welfare. Oh, my prince! recall that terrible hour in which we separated. I said to you that I had betrothed myself to

Captain du Trouffle—that of my own free choice, and influenced by love alone, I gave myself to him."

"I remember that hour."

"Well, then, in that hour we were not alone. The king was concealed behind the portiere, and listened to my words. He dictated them!—he threatened me with destruction if I betrayed his presence by look or word; if I gave you reason to suspect that I did not, of my own choice and lovingly, give myself to this unloved, yes, this hated man! I yielded only after the most fearful contest with the king, to whom, upon my knees and bathed in tears, I pleaded for pity."

"What means could the king use, what threats could he utter, which forced you to such a step?" said the prince, incredulously. "Did he threaten you with death if you did not obey? When one truly loves, death has no terrors! Did he say he would murder me if you did not release me? You knew I had a strong arm and a stronger will; you should have trusted both. You placed your fate in my hands; you should have obeyed no other commands than mine. And now shall I speak the whole truth? I do not believe in this sacrifice on your part; it would have required more than mortal strength, and it would have been cruel in the extreme. You saw what I suffered. My heart was torn with anguish! No, madame, no; you did not make this sacrifice, or, if you did, you loved me not. If you had loved me, you could not have seen me suffer so cruelly, you would have told the truth, even in the presence of the king. No earthly power can control true love; she is self-sustained and makes her own laws. No! no! I do not believe in this offering; and you make this excuse either to heal my sick heart, or because your pride is mortified at my want of consideration; you wish to recover my good opinion."

"Alas! alas! he does not believe me," cried Louise.

"No, I do not believe you," said the prince, kindly; "and yet you must not think that I am still angry. I not only forgive, but I thank you. It is to you, indeed, Louise, that I owe my present happiness, all those noble and pure joys which a true love bestows. I thank you for this—you and the king. It was wise in the king to deny me that which I then thought essential to my happiness, but which would, at last, have brought us both to shame and to despair. The love, which must shun the light of day and hide itself in obscurity, pales, and withers, and dies. Happy love must have the sunlight of heaven and God's blessing upon it! All this failed in our case, and it was a blessing for us both that you saw it clearly, and resigned a doubtful happiness at my side for surer peace with Monsieur du Trouffle. From my soul I thank you, Louise. See what a costly treasure has bloomed for me from the grave of my betrayed love. Look at that lovely young woman who, although disguised as a shepherdess, stands out in the midst of all other women, an imperial queen! a queen of beauty, grace, and fascination! This charming, innocent, and modest young woman belongs to me; she is my wife; and I have your inconstancy to thank you for this rare gem. Oh, madame, I have indeed reason to forgive you for the past, to be grateful to you as long as I live. But for you I should never have married the Princess Wilhelmina. What no menaces, no entreaties, no commands of the king could accomplish, your faithlessness effected. I married! God, in his goodness, chose you to be a mediator between me and my fate; it was His will that, from your hand, I should receive my life's blessing. You cured me of a wandering and unworthy passion, that I might feel the truth and enjoy the blessing of a pure love, and a love which now fills my heart and soul, my thoughts, my existence for my darling wife."

"Ah, you are very cruel," said Louise, scarcely able to suppress her tears of rage.

"I am only true, madame," said the prince, smiling. "You wished to know of me if I were still angry with you, and I reply that I have not only forgiven, but I bless your inconstancy. And now, I pray you let us end this conversation, which I will never renew. Let the past die and be buried! We have both of us commenced a new life under the sunshine of a new love; we will not allow any cloud of remembrances to cast a shadow upon it. Look, the beautiful shepherdesses are seeking flowers in the meadows, and my wife stands alone upon the borders of the lake. Allow me to join her, if only to see if the clear waters of the lake reflect back her image as lovely and enchanting as the reality."

The prince bowed, and with hasty steps took the path that led to the lake.

Louise looked at him scornfully. "He despises me and he loves her fondly; but she—does the princess love him?—not so! her glance is cold, icy, when she looks upon him; and to-day I saw her turn pale as the prince approached her. No, she loves him not; but who then—who? she is young, ardent, and, it appears to me, impressible; she cannot live without love. I will find out; a day will come when I will take vengeance for this hour. I await that day!"

While Louise forced herself to appear gay, in order to meet her husband without embarrassment, and the prince walked hastily onward, the princess stood separated from her ladies, on the borders of the lake, with the Count Kalkreuth at her side. The count had been appointed her cavalier for the day, by the prince her husband; she seemed to give her undivided attention to the swans, who were floating before her, and stretching out their graceful necks to receive food from her hands. As she bowed down to feed the swans, she whispered lightly, "Listen, count, to what I have to say to you. If possible, laugh merrily, that my ladies may hear; let your countenance be gay, for I see the prince approaching. In ten minutes he will be with us; do you understand my low tones?"

"I understand you, princess; alas! I fear I understand without words; I have read my sentence in the eyes of your husband. The prince suspects me."

"No," said she, sadly bowing down and plucking a few violets, which she threw to the swans; "he has no suspicion, but he loves me."

The count sprang back as if wounded. "He loves you!" he cried, in a loud, almost threatening tone. "For pity's sake speak low," said the princess. "Look, the ladies turn toward us, and are listening curiously, and you have frightened the swans from the shore. Laugh, I pray you; speak a few loud and jesting words, count, I implore you."

"I cannot," said the count. "Command me to throw myself into the lake and I will obey you joyfully, and in dying I will call your name and bless it; but do not ask me to smile when you tell me that the prince loves you."

"Yes, he loves me; he confessed it to-day," said the princess, shuddering. "Oh, it was a moment of inexpressible horror; a moment in which that became a sin which, until then, had been pure and innocent. So long as my husband did not love me, or ask my love, I was free to bestow it where I would and when I would; so soon as he loves me, and demands my love, I am a culprit if I refuse it."

"And I false to my friend," murmured Kalkreuth.

"We must instantly separate," whispered she. "We must bury our love out of our sight, which until now has lived purely and modestly in our hearts, and this must be its funeral procession. You see I have already begun to deck the grave with flowers, and that tears are consecrating them." She pointed with her jewelled hand to the bouquet of white camelias which adorned her bosom.

"It was cruel not to wear my flowers," said the count. "Was it not enough to crush me?—must you also trample my poor flowers, consecrated with my kisses and my whispers, under your feet?"

"The red roses which you gave me," said she, lightly, "I will keep as a remembrance of the beautiful and glorious dream which the rude reality of life has dissipated. These camelias are superb, but without fragrance, and colorless as my sad features. I must wear them, for my husband gave them to me, and in so doing I decorate the grave of my love. Farewell!—hereafter I will live for my duties; as I cannot accept your love, I will merit your highest respect. Farewell, and if from this time onward we are cold and strange, never forget that our souls belong to each other, and when I dare no longer think of the past, I will pray for you."

"You never loved me," whispered the count, with pallid, trembling lips, "or you could not give me up so rashly; you would not have the cruel courage to spurn me from you. You are weary of me, and since the prince loves you, you despise the poor humble heart which laid itself at your feet. Yes, yes, I cannot compete with this man, who is a prince and the brother of a king; who—"

"Who is my husband," cried she, proudly, "and who, while he loves me, dares ask that I shall accept his love."

"Ah, now you are angry with me," stammered the count; "you—"

"Hush!" whispered she, "do you not see the prince? Do laugh! Bow down and give the swans these flowers!"

The count took the flowers, and as he gave them to the swans, he whispered:

"Give me at least a sign that you are not angry, and that you do not love the prince. Throw this hated bouquet, which has taken the place of mine, into the water; it is like a poisoned arrow in my heart."

"Hush!" whispered the princess. She turned and gave the prince a friendly welcome.

Prince Henry was so happy in her presence, and so dazzled by her beauty, that he did not remark the melancholy of the count, and spoke with him gayly and jestingly, while the count mastered himself, and replied in the same spirit.

The princess bowed down to the swans, whom she enticed once more with caresses to the borders of the lake. Suddenly she uttered a loud cry, and called to the two gentlemen for help. The great white swan had torn the camelias from the bosom of the princess, and sailed off proudly upon the clear waters of the lake.

CHAPTER V
INTRIGUES

While Prince Henry celebrated Arcadian fetes at Rheinsberg, and gave himself up to love and joy, King Frederick lived in philosophic retirement at Sans-Souci. He came to Berlin only to visit the queen-mother, now dangerously ill, or to attend the meetings of his cabinet ministers. Never had the king lived so quietly, never had he received so few guests at Sans-Souci, and, above all, never had the world so little cause to speak of the King of Prussia. He appeared content with the laurels which the two Silesian wars had placed upon his heroic brow, and he only indulged the wish that Europe, exhausted by her long and varied wars, would allow him that rest and peace which the world at large seemed to enjoy. Those who were honored with invitations to Sans-Souci, and had opportunities to see the king, could only speak of that earthly paradise; of the peaceful stillness which reigned there, and which was reflected in every countenance; of Frederick's calm cheerfulness and innocent enjoyment.

"The king thinks no more of politics," said the frolicsome Berliners; "he is absorbed in the arts and sciences, and, above all other things, he lives to promote the peaceful prosperity of his people." The balance of power and foreign relations troubled him no longer; he wished for no conquests, and thought not of war. In the morning he was occupied with scientific works, wrote in his "Histoire de mon Temps," or to his friends, and took part in the daily-recurring duties of the government. The remainder of the day was passed in the garden of Sans-Souci, in pleasant walks and animated conversation, closing always with music. Concerts took place every evening in the apartments of the king, in which he took part, and he practised difficult pieces of his own or Quantz's composition, under Quantz's direction. From time to time he was much occupied with his picture-gallery, and sent Gotzkowsky to Italy to purchase the paintings of the celebrated masters.

King Frederick appeared to have reached his goal; at least, that which, during the storm of war, he had often called his ideal; he could devote his life to philosophy and art in the enchanting retirement of his beloved Sans-Souci. The tumult and discord of the world did not trouble him; in fact, the whole world seemed to be at peace, and all Europe was glad and happy.

Maria Theresa was completely bound by the last peace contract at Dresden; besides, the two Silesian wars had weakened and impoverished Austria, and time was necessary to heal her wounds before she dared make a new attempt to reconquer the noble jewel of Silesia, which Frederick had torn from her crown. Notwithstanding her pious and Christian pretensions, she hated Frederick with her whole heart.

England had allied herself with Russia. France was at the moment too much occupied with the pageants which the lovely Marquise de Pompadour celebrated at Versailles, not to be in peace and harmony with all the world; yes, even with her natural enemy, Austria. Count Kaunitz, her ambassador at Paris, had, by his wise and adroit conduct, banished the cloud of mistrust which had so long lowered between these two powers.

This was the state of things at the close of the year 1775. Then was the general quiet interrupted by the distant echo of a cannon. Europe was startled, and rose up from her comfortable siesta to listen and inquire after the cause of this significant thunderbolt. This roar of cannon, whose echo only had been heard, had its birth far, far away in America. The cannon, however, had been fired by a European power—by England, always distinguished for her calculating selfishness, which she wished the world to consider praiseworthy and honorable policy. England considered her mercantile interests in America endangered by France, and she thirsted with desire to have not only an East India but a West India company. The French colonies in America had long excited the envy and covetousness of England, and as a sufficient cause for war had utterly failed, she was bold enough to take the initiative without excuse!

In the midst of a general peace, and without any declaration of war, she seized upon a country lying on the borders of the Ohio River, and belonging to French Canada, made an attack upon some hundred merchant-ships, which were navigating the Ohio, under the protection of the ships-of-war, and took them as prizes. [Footnote: *"Characteristics of the Important Events of the Seven Years' War," by Retson.*]

That was the cannon-shot which roused all Europe from her comfortable slumber and dreamy rest.

The Empress of Austria began to make warlike preparations in Bohemia, and to assemble her troops on the borders of Saxony and Bohemia. The Empress of Russia discontinued instantaneously her luxurious feasts and wild orgies, armed her soldiers, and placed them on the borders of Courland. She formed an immediate alliance with England, by which she bound herself to protect the territory of George II. in Germany, if attacked by France, in retaliation for the French merchant-ships taken by England on the Ohio River. Hanover, however, was excepted, as Frederick of Prussia might possibly give her his aid. For this promised aid, Russia received from England the sum of 150,000 pounds sterling, which was truly welcome to the powerful Bestuchef, from, the extravagant and pomp-loving minister of the queen.

Saxony also prepared for war, and placed her army on the borders of Prussia, for which she received a subsidy from Austria. This was as gladly welcomed by Count Bruhl, the luxurious minister of King Augustus the Third of Poland and Saxony, as the English subsidy was by Bestuchef.

The King of France appeared to stand alone; even as completely alone as Frederick of Prussia. Every eye therefore was naturally fixed upon these two powers, who seemed thus forced by fate to extend the hand of fellowship to each other, and form such an alliance as England had done with Russia, and Austria with Saxony.

This contract between Prussia and France would have been the signal for a general war, for which all the powers of Europe were now arming themselves. But France did not extend her hand soon enough to obtain the friendship of Prussia. France distrusted Prussia, even as Austria, England, Russia, and Saxony distrusted and feared the adroit young adventurer, who in the last fifty years had placed himself firmly amongst the great powers of Europe, and was bold, brave, and wise enough to hold a powerful and self-sustained position in their circle.

France—that is to say, Louis the Fifteenth—France—that is to say, the Marquise de Pompadour, hated the King of Prussia manfully. By his bold wit he had often brought the French court and its immoralities into ridicule and contempt.

Austria and her minister Kaunitz and Maria Theresa hated Frederick of Prussia, because of his conquest of Silesia.

Russia—that is to say, Elizabeth and Bestuchef—hated the King of Prussia for the same reason with France. Frederick's cutting wit had scourged the manners of the Russian court, as it had humiliated and exposed the court of France.

Saxony—that is to say, Augustus the Third, and his minister, Count Bruhl—hated Frederick from instinct, from envy, from resentment. This insignificant and small neighbor had spread her wings and made so bold a flight, that Saxony was completely over-shadowed.

England hated no one, but she feared Prussia and France, and this fear led her to master the old-rooted national hatred to Russia, and form an alliance with her for mutual protection. But the English people did not share the fears of their king; they murmured over this Russian ally, and this discontent, which found expression in Parliament, rang so loudly, that Frederick might well have heard it, and formed his own conclusions as to the result. But did he hear it? Was the sound of his flute so loud? Was his study hermetically sealed, so that no echo from the outside world could reach his ears?

There was no interruption to his quiet, peaceful life; he hated nobody, made no warlike preparations; his soldiers exercised no more than formerly. Truly they exercised; and at the first call to battle, 150,000 men would be under arms.

But Frederick seemed not inclined to give this call; not inclined to exchange the calm pleasures of Sans-Souci for the rude noises of tents and battle-fields. He seemed to be in peaceful harmony with all nations. He was particularly friendly and conciliating toward the Austrian embassy; and not only was the ambassador, Count Peubla invited often to the royal table, but his secretary, Baron Weingarten came also to Potsdam and Sans-Souci. The king appeared attached to him, and encouraged him to come often, to walk in the royal gardens.

Frederick was gracious and kind toward the officials of all the German powers. On one occasion, when the wife of Councillor Reichart, attached to the Saxon embassy, was confined, at Frederick's earnest wish, his private secretary, Eichel, stood as god-father to the child. *[Footnote: "Characteristics of the Important Events of the Seven Years' War."]*

In order to promote good feeling in Saxony, the king sent Count Mattzahn, one of the most eloquent cavaliers of the day, to the Dresden court; and so well supplied was he, that he dared compete in pomp and splendor with Count Bruhl.

Frederick appeared to attach special importance to the friendship of Saxony, and with none of his foreign ambassadors was he engaged in so active a correspondence as with Mattzahn. It was said that these letters were of a harmless and innocent nature, relating wholly to paintings, which the count was to purchase from the Saxon galleries, or to music, which Frederick wished to obtain from amongst the collection of the dead Hesse, or to an Italian singer Frederick wished to entice to Berlin.

The world no longer favored Frederick's retirement. The less disposed he was to mingle in politics, the more Maria Theresa, Elizabeth of Russia, Augustus of Saxony, and the Marquise de Pompadour agitated the subject.

France had not forgotten that the contract between herself and Prussia was about to expire. She knew also that the subsidy money between England

and Russia had not yet been voted by Parliament. It was therefore possible to reap some advantages from this point. With this view, France sent the Duke de Nivernois as special ambassador to Berlin, to treat with the king as to the renewal of the old alliance.

The Duke de Nivernois came with a glittering suite to Berlin, and was received at the Prussian court with all the consideration which his rank and official character demanded. The grand master of ceremonies, Baron von Pollnitz, was sent forward to meet him, and to invite him, in the name of the king, to occupy one of the royal palaces in Berlin.

Every room of the palace was splendidly decorated for the reception of the duke, and as soon as he arrived, two guards were placed before the house—a mark of consideration which the king had only heretofore given to reigning princes.

The duke accepted these distinguished attentions with lively gratitude, and pleaded for an immediate audience, in order to present his credentials.

Pollnitz was commissioned to make all necessary arrangements, and agree with the duke as to the day and hour of the ceremony.

The king, who wished to give the French duke a proof of his consideration, intended that the presentation should be as imposing as possible, and all Berlin was to be witness of the friendship existing between the French and Prussian courts.

Upon the appointed day, a dazzling assemblage of equipages stood before the palace of the Duke de Nivernois. These were the royal festal carriages, intended for the members of the French embassy. Then followed a long line of carriages, occupied by the distinguished members of the Prussian court. Slowly and solemnly this pompous procession moved through the streets, and was received at the portal of the king's palace by the royal guard. Richly-dressed pages, in advance of whom stood the grand master of ceremonies with his golden staff, conducted the French ambassador to the White saloon, where the king, in all his royal pomp, and surrounded by the princes of his house, received him.

The solemn ceremony began; the duke drew near the throne, and, bowing his knee, handed his credentials to the king, who received them with a gracious smile.

The duke commenced his address; it was filled with flowery phrases, suited to the great occasion. Frederick listened with the most earnest attention, and his reply was kind, but dignified and laconic.

The public ceremony was over, and now came the important part of the audience, the confidential conversation. To this point the duke had looked with lively impatience; for this, indeed, had he been sent to Berlin.

The king descended from the throne, and laying aside all the solemnity of court etiquette, he approached the duke in the most gracious and genial manner, welcomed him heartily, and expressed his sincere delight at his arrival.

"Ah, sire," said the duke, with animation, "how happy will my king be to learn that his ambassador has been so graciously received by your majesty!"

The king smiled. "I thought the ceremony was all over," said he, "and that I no longer spoke with the ambassador, but with the Duke de Nivernois, whom I know and love, and whose intellectual conversation will afford me a rare pleasure. Let us, therefore, chat together innocently, and forget the stiff ceremonies with which, I think, we have both been sufficiently burdened today. Tell me something of Paris, monsieur, of that lovely, enchanting, but overbold coquette, Paris, whom the world adores while it ridicules, and imitates while it blames."

"Ah, sire, if I must speak of Paris, I must first tell you of my king—of my king, who wishes nothing more ardently than the renewal of the bond of friendship between your majesty and himself, and the assurance of its long continuance, who—"

"That is most kind of his majesty," said Frederick, interrupting him, "and I certainly share the friendly wishes of my exalted brother of France. But tell me now something of your learned men. How goes it with the Academy? Do they still refuse Voltaire a seat, while so many unknown men have become academicians?"

"Yes, sire these academicians are obstinate in their conclusions, and, as the Academy is a sort of republic, the king has no power to control them If that were not so, my exalted master, King Louis, in order to be agreeable to your majesty, would exert all his influence, and—"

"Ah, sir," interrupted the king, "it is just and beautiful that the Academy is a free republic, which will not yield to the power and influence of the king. Art and science need for their blossom and growth freedom of thought and speech. Fate ordained that I should be born a king, but when alone in my study, alone with my books, I am fully content to be republican in the kingdom of letters. I confess the truth to you when, as a wise republican, I read thoughtfully in the pages of history, I sometimes come to the conclusion that kings and princes are unnecessary articles of luxury, and I shrug my shoulders at them rather contemptuously."

"And yet, sire, the arts need the protection of princes; that the republic of letters blooms and flourishes in a monarchy is shown in Prussia, where a royal republican and a republican king governs his people, and at the same time gives freedom of thought and speech to science. France should be proud and happy that your majesty has adopted so many of her sons into your republic of letters; we dare, therefore, come to the conclusion that your majesty will not confine your interest wholly to them, but that this alliance between France and Prussia, which my king so earnestly desires and—"

"Unhappily," said the king, interrupting him eagerly, "the distinguished Frenchmen who have become my allies, are exactly those whom their strong-minded, fanatical mother, La France, has cast out from her bosom as dishonored sons. Voltaire lives in Ferney. Jean Jacques Rousseau, whom I admire but do not love, lives in Geneva, where he has been obliged to take refuge. I have also been told that the pension which, in a favorable moment, was granted to D'Alembert, has been withdrawn. Have I been falsely informed? has my friend D'Alembert not fallen into disgrace? is not my friend the encyclopaedian, regarded as a transgressor, and a high traitor because he uses the undoubted right of free thought, does not blindly believe, but looks abroad with open eyes and a clear intellect?"

The duke replied by a few confused and disconnected words, and a shadow fell upon his clear countenance; three times had Frederick interrupted him when he sought to speak of the King of France and his friendship for his brother of Prussia. The duke did not dare choose this theme for the fourth time, which was so evidently distasteful to the king; he must, therefore, submit and follow the lead of his majesty, and in lieu of alliances and state questions discuss philosophy and the arts. So soon as the duke came to this conclusion, he smoothed his brow, and, with all his amiability, animation, and intelligence, he replied to the questions of the king, and the conversation was carried on in an unbroken stream of wit and gayety.

"At the next audience I will surely find an opportunity to speak of politics," said the duke to himself. "The king cannot always be an immovable as to-day."

But the second and the third audience came, and the king was as inexplicable as the first time; he conversed with the duke kindly and freely showed him the most marked attention and personal confidence; but so often as the duke sought to introduce the subject of politics and the public interests which had brought him to Berlin, the king interrupted him and led the conversation to indifferent subjects. This lasted two weeks, and the French court looked with painful anxiety for intelligence from the Duke de Nivernois that the old alliance was renewed and fully ratified, and she had, therefore, nothing to fear from Prussia. This uncertainty was no longer to be borne, and the duke determined to end it by a coup d'etat.

He wrote, therefore, to the king, and asked for a private audience. To his great joy his request was granted; the king invited him to come the next day to Sans-Souci. "At last! at last!" said the duke, drawing a long breath; and with proud, French assurance, he added, "To-morrow, then, we will renew this contract which binds the hands of Prussia, and gives France liberty of action."

CHAPTER VI
THE PRIVATE AUDIENCE

The king received the French ambassador without ceremony. There were no guards, no pages, no swarms of curious listening courtiers, only a few of his trusty friends, who welcomed the duke and conversed with him, while Pollnitz entered the adjoining room and informed the king of his arrival.

"His majesty entreats the duke to enter." said Pollnitz, opening the door of the library. The king advanced. He was dressed simply; even the golden star, which was seldom absent from his coat, was now missing.

"Come, duke," said the king, pleasantly, "come into my tusculum." He then entered the library, quickly followed by the duke.

"Well, sir," said the king, "we are now in that room in which I lately told you I was but a republican. You have crossed the threshold of the republic of letters!"

"But I see a king before me," said the duke, bowing reverentially; "a king who has vanquished his republic, and surpassed all the great spirits that have gone before him."

The king's glance rested upon the shelves filled with books, on whose back glittered in golden letters the most distinguished names of all ages.

"Homer, Tacitus, Livy, Petrarch!—ye great spirits of my republic! hear how this traitor slanders you."

"How I honor you, sire, for truly it is a great honor to be subdued and vanquished by such a king as Frederick the Second."

The king looked at him fixedly. "You wish to bewilder me with flattery, duke," said he, "well knowing that it is a sweet opiate, acceptable to princes, generally causing their ruin. But in this chamber, duke, I am safe from this danger, and here in my republic we will both enjoy the Spartan soup of truth. Believe me, sir, it is at times a wholesome dish, though to the pampered stomach it is bitter and distasteful. I can digest it, and as you have come to visit me, you will have to partake of it."

"And I crave it, sire—crave it as a man who has fasted for two weeks."

"For two weeks?" said the king, laughing. "Ah, it is true you have been here just that time."

"For two long weeks has your majesty kept me fasting and longing for this precious soup," said the duke, reproachfully.

"My broth was not ready," said the king, gayly; "it was still bubbling in the pot. It is now done, and we will consume it together. Let us be seated, duke."

If Frederick had turned at this moment, he would have seen the grand chamberlain Pollnitz advancing on tiptoe to the open door, in order to listen to the conversation. But the king was looking earnestly at the ambassador. After a few moments of silence, he turned to the duke.

"Is my soup still too hot for you?" said he, laughingly.

"No, sire," said the duke, bowing. "But I waited for your majesty to take the first spoonful. Would it not be better to close that door?"

"No," said the king, hastily; "I left it open, intentionally, so that your eyes, when wearied with the gloom of my republic, could refresh themselves on the glittering costumes of my courtiers."

"He left it open," thought the duke, "for these courtiers to hear all that is said. He wishes the whole world to know how he rejected the friendship of France."

"Well," said the king, "I will take my spoonful. We will commence without further delay. Duke de Nivernois, you are here because the contract made between France and Prussia is at an end, and because France wishes me to fancy that she is anxious for a renewal of this treaty, and for the friendship of Prussia."

"France wishes to convince you of this, sire," said the duke.

"Convince me?" said the king, ironically. "And how?"

"King Louis of France not only proposes to renew this contract, she, who he wishes to draw the bonds of friendship much closer between France and Prussia."

"And to what end?" said the king. "For you well know, duke, that in politics personal inclinations must not be considered. Were it not so, I would, without further delay, grasp the friendly hand that my brother of France extends toward me, for the whole world knows that I love France, and am proud of the friendship of her great spirits. But as, unfortunately, there is no talk here of personal inclinations but of politics, I repeat my question. To what end does France desire the friendship of Prussia? What am I to pay for it? You see, duke, I am a bad diplomatist—I make no digression, but go to the point at once."

"And that, perhaps, is the nicest diplomacy," said the duke, sighing.

"But, duke, do tell me, why is France so anxious for the friendship of Prussia?"

"To have an ally in you and be your ally. By the first, France will have a trusty and powerful friend in Germany when her lands are attacked by the King of England; by the last, your majesty will have a trusty and powerful friend when Prussia is attacked by Russia or Austria."

"We will now speak of the first," said the king, quietly. "France, then, thinks to transplant this war with England to German ground?"

"Everywhere, sire, that the English colors predominate. England alone will be accountable for this war."

"It is true England has been hard upon you, but still it seems to me you have revenged yourselves sufficiently. When England made herself supreme ruler of the Ohio, France, by the conquest of the Isle of Minorca, obtained dominion over the Mediterranean Sea, thereby wounding England so deeply, that in her despair she turned her weapons against herself. Admiral Byng, having been overcome by your admiral Marquis de la Gallissionaire, paid for it with his life. I think France should be satisfied with this expiation."

"France will wash off her insults in English blood, and Minorca is no compensation for Canada and Ohio. England owes us satisfaction, and we will obtain it in Hanover."

"In Hanover?" repeated the king, angrily.

"Hanover will be ours, sire, though we had no such ally as Germany; but it will be ours the sooner if we have that help which you can give us. Standing between two fires, England will have to succumb, there will be no escape for her. That is another advantage, sire, that France expects from the treaty with Prussia. But I will now speak of the advantages which your majesty may expect from this alliance. You are aware that Prussia is surrounded by threatening enemies; that Austria and Russia are approaching her borders with evil intentions, and that a day may soon come when Maria Theresa may wish to reconquer this Silesia which, in her heart, she still calls her own. When this time comes, your majesty will not be alone; your ally,

France, will be at your side; she will repay with faithful, active assistance the services which your majesty rendered her in Hanover. She will not only render her all the assistance in her power, but she will also allow her to partake of the advantages of this victory. Hanover is a rich land, not rich only in products, but in many other treasures. The Electors of Hanover have in their residences not only their chests filled with gold and precious jewels, but also the most magnificent paintings. It is but natural that we should pay ourselves in Hanover for the expenses of this war of which England is the cause. You, then, will share with us these treasures. And still this is not all. France is grateful; she offers you, therefore, one of her colonies, the Isle of Tobago, as a pledge of friendship and love."

"Where is this isle?" said the king, quietly.

"In the West Indies, sire."

"And where is Hanover?"

The duke looked at the king in amazement, and remained silent.

The king repeated his question.

"Well," said the duke, hesitatingly, "Hanover is in Germany."

"And for this German land which, with my aid, France is to conquer, I am to receive as a reward the little Isle of Tobago in the West Indies! Have you finished, dyke, or have you other propositions to make?"

"Sire, I have finished, and await your answer."

"And this answer, duke, shall be clearer and franker than your questions. I will begin by answering the latter part of your speech. Small and insignificant as the King of Prussia may appear in your eyes, I would have you know he is no robber, no highwayman; he leaves these brilliant amusements without envy to France. And now, my dear duke, I must inform you, that since this morning it has been placed out of my power to accept this alliance; for this morning a treaty was signed, by which I became the ally of England!"

"It is impossible, sire," cried the duke; "this cannot be!"

"Not possible, sir!" said the king, "and still it is true. I have formed a treaty with England—this matter is settled! I have been an ally of Louis XV.; I have nothing to complain of in him. I love him; well, am I now his enemy? I hope that there may be a time when I may again approach the King of France. Pray tell him how anxiously I look forward to this time. Tell him I am much attached to him."

"Ah, sire," said the duke, sighing, "it is a great misfortune. I dare not go to my monarch with this sad, unexpected news; my monarch who loves you so tenderly, whose most earnest wish it is for France to be allied to Prussia."

"Ah, duke," said Frederick, laughing, "France wishes for ships as allies. I have none to offer—England has. With her help I shall keep the Russians from Prussia, and with the aid she will keep the French from Hanover."

"We are to be enemies, then?" said the duke, sadly.

"It is a necessary evil, for which there is no remedy. But Louis XV. can form other alliances," said Frederick, ironically. "It may be for his interest to unite with the house of Austria!"

The duke was much embarrassed.

"Your majesty is not in earnest," said he, anxiously.

"Why not, duke?" said Frederick; "an alliance between France and Austria—it sounds very natural. If I were in your place, I would propose this to my court."

He now rose, which was a sign to the duke that the audience was at an end.

"I must now send a courier at once to my court," said the duke, "and I will not fail to state that your majesty advises us to unite with Austria."

"You will do well; that is," said the king, with a meaning smile—"that is, if you think your court is in need of such advice, and has not already acted without it. When do you leave, duke?"

"To-morrow morning, sire."

"Farewell, duke, and do not forget that in my heart I am the friend of France, though we meet as enemies on the battle-field."

The duke bowed reverentially, and, sighing deeply, left the royal library, "the republic of letters," to hasten to Berlin.

The king looked after him thoughtfully.

"The die is cast," said he, softly. "There will be war. Our days of peace and quietude are over, and the days of danger are approaching!"

CHAPTER VII
THE TRAITOR

The sun had just risen, and was shedding its golden rays over the garden of Sans-Souci, decking the awaking flowers with glittering dew-drops. All was quiet—Nature alone was up and doing; no one was to be seen, no sound was to be heard, but the rustling of trees and the chirping of birds. All was still and peaceful; it seemed as if the sound of human misery and passion could not reach this spot. There was something so holy in this garden, that you could but believe it to be a part of paradise in which the serpent had not yet exercised his arts of seduction. But no, this is but a beautiful dream. Man is here, but he is sleeping; he is still resting from the toils and sorrows of the past day. Man is here—he is coming to destroy the peacefulness of Nature with his sorrows and complaints.

The little gate at the farthest end of that shady walk is opened, and a man enters. The dream is at an end, and Sans-Souci is now but a beautiful garden, not a paradise, for it has been desecrated by the foot of man. He hastens up the path leading to the palace; he hurries forward, panting and gasping. His face is colorless, his long hair is fluttering in the morning wind, his eyes are fixed and glaring; his clothes are covered with dust, and his head is bare.

There is something terrifying in the sudden appearance of this man. Nature seems to smile no more since he came; the trees have stopped their whispering, the birds cannot continue their melodious songs since they have seen his wild, anxious look. The peacefulness of Nature is broken. For man—that is to say, misery, misfortune; for man—that is to say, sin, guilt, and meanness—is there, pouring destroying drops of poison in the golden chalice of creation.

Breathlessly he hurries on, looking neither to right nor left. He has now reached the terrace, and now he stops for a moment to recover breath. He sees not the glorious panorama lying at his feet; he is blind to all but himself. He is alone in the world—alone with his misery, his pain. Now he hastens on to the back of the palace. The sentinels walking before the back and the front of the castle know him, know where he is going, and they barely glance at him as he knocks long and loudly at that little side window.

It is opened, and a young girl appears, who, when perceiving this pale, anxious countenance, which is striving in vain to smile at her, cries out loudly, and folds her hands as if in prayer.

"Hush!" said he, roughly; "hush! let me in."

"Some misfortune has happened!" said she, terrified.

"Yes, Rosa, a great misfortune, but let me in, if you do not wish to ruin me."

The young girl disappears, and the man hastens to the side door of the castle. It is opened, and he slips in.

Perfect peace reigns once more in the garden of Sans-Souci. Nature is now smiling, for she is alone with her innocence. Man is not there! But now, in the castle, in the dwelling of the castle warder, and in the room of his lovely daughter Rosa, all is alive. There is whispering, and weeping, and sighing, and praying; there is Rosa, fearful and trembling, her face covered with tears, and opposite her, her pale, woe-begone lover.

"I have been walking all night," said he, with a faint and hollow voice. "I did not know that Berlin was so far from Potsdam, and had I known it, I would not have dared to take a wagon or a horse; I had to slip away very quietly. While by Count Puebla's order my room was guarded, and I thought to be in it, I descended into the garden by the grape-vine, which reached up to my window. The gardener had no suspicion of how I came there, when I required him to unlock the door, but laughed cunningly, thinking I was bound to some rendezvous. And so I wandered on in fear and pain, in despair and anger, and it seemed to me as if the road would never come to an end. At times I stopped, thinking I heard behind me wild cries and curses, the stamping of horses, and the rolling of wheels; but it was imagination. Ah! it was a frightful road; but it is past. But now I will be strong, for this concerns my name, my life, my honor. Why do you laugh, Rosa?" said he, angrily; "do you dare to laugh, because I speak of my name—my honor?"

"I did not laugh," said Rosa, looking with terror at the disturbed countenance of her lover.

"Yes, you laughed, and you were right to laugh, when I spoke of my honor; I who have no honor; I who have shamed my name; I upon whose brow is the sign of murder: for I am guilty of the ruin of a man, and the chains on his hands are cursing my name."

"My God! He is mad," murmured Rosa.

"No, I am not mad," said he, with a heart-breaking smile. "I know all, all! Were I mad, I would not be so unhappy. Were I unconscious, I would suffer less. But, no, I remember all. I know how this evil commenced, how it grew and poisoned my heart. The evil was my poverty, my covetousness, and perhaps also my ambition. I was not content to bear forever the chains of bondage; I wished to be free from want. I determined it should no more be said that the sisters of Count Weingarten had to earn their bread by their needlework, while he feasted sumptuously at the royal table. This it was that caused my ruin. These frightful words buzzed in my ears so long, that in my despair I determined to stop them at any price, and so I committed my first crime, and received a golden reward for my treason. My sisters did not work now; I bought a small house for them, and gave them all that I received. I shuddered at the sight of this money; I would keep none of it. I was again the poor secretary Weingarten, but my family was not helpless; they had nothing to fear."

To whom was he telling all this? Certainly not to that young girl standing before him, pale and trembling. He had forgotten himself; he had forgotten her whom in other days he had called his heart's darling.

As she sank at his feet and covered his hands with her tears, he rose hastily from his seat; he now remembered that he was not alone.

"What have I said?" cried he, wildly. "Why do you weep?"

"I weep because you have forgotten me," said she, softly; "I weep because, in accusing yourself, you make no excuse for your crime; not even your love for your poor Rosa."

"It is true," said he, sadly, "I had forgotten our love. And still it is the only excuse that I have for my second crime. I had determined to be a good man, and to expiate my one crime throughout my whole life. But when I saw you, your beauty fascinated me, and you drew me on. I went with open eyes into the net which you prepared for me, Rosa. I allowed myself to be allured by your beauty, knowing well that it would draw me into a frightful abyss."

"Ah," said Rosa, groaning, "how cruelly you speak of our love!"

"Of our love!" repeated he, shrugging his shoulders. "Child, in this hour we will be true to each other. Ours was no true love. You were in love with my noble name and position—I with your youth, your beauty, your coquettish ways. Our souls were not in unison. You gave yourself to me, not because you loved me, but because you wished to deceive me. I allowed myself to be deceived because of your loveliness and because I saw the golden reward which your deceitful love would bring me."

"You are cruel and unjust," said Rosa, sadly. "It may be true that you never loved me, but I loved you truly. I gave you my whole heart."

"Yes, and in giving it," said he, harshly—"in giving it you had the presence of mind to keep the aim of your tenderness always in view. While your arms were around me, your little hand which seemed to rest upon my heart, sought for the key which I always kept in my vest-pocket, and which I had lately told you belonged to the desk in which the important papers of the embassy were placed. You found this key, Rosa, and I knew it, but I only laughed, and pressed you closer to my heart."

"Terrible! terrible!" said Rosa, trembling. "He knew all, and still he let me do it!"

"Yes I allowed you to do it—I did not wish to be better than the girl I loved: and, as she desired to deceive me, I let myself be deceived. I allowed it, because the demon of gold had taken possession of me. I took the important papers out of my desk, to which you had stolen the key, and hid them. Then the tempters came and whispered of golden rewards, of eternal gratitude, of fortune, honor; and these fiendish whispers misled my soul. I sold my honor and became a traitor, and all this for the sake of gold! So I became what I now am. I do not reproach you Rosa, for most likely it would have happened without you."

"But what danger threatens you now?" asked Rosa.

"The just punishment for a traitor," said he, hoarsely. "Give me some wine, Rosa, so that I can gain strength to go to the king at once."

"To the king at this early hour?"

"And why not? Have I not been with him often at this hour, when I had important news or dispatches to give him? So give me the wine, Rosa."

Rosa left the room, but returned almost instantly. He took the bottle from her and filled a glass hastily.

"Now," said he, breathing deeply, "I feel that I live again. My blood flows freely through my veins, and my heart is beating loudly. Now to the king!"

He stood before a glass for a moment to arrange his hair; then pressed a cold kiss upon Rosa's pale, trembling lips, and left the room. With a firm, sure tread, he hurried through the halls and chambers. No one stopped him, for no one was there to see him. In the king's antechamber sat Deesen taking his breakfast.

"Is the king up?" asked Weingarten.

"The sun has been up for hours, and so of course the king is up," said Deesen, proudly.

"Announce me to his majesty; I have some important news for him."

He entered the king's chamber, and returned in a few moments for Weingarten.

The king was sitting in an arm-chair by a window, which he had opened to breathe the fresh summer air. His white greyhound, Amalthea, lay at his feet, looking up at him with his soft black eyes. In his right hand the king held his flute.

"You are early, sir," said he, turning to Weingarten. "You must have very important news."

"Yes, sire, very important," said Weingarten, approaching nearer.

The king reached out his hand. "Give them to me," said he.

"Sire, I have no dispatches."

"A verbal message, then. Speak."

"Sire, all is lost; Count Puebla suspects me."

The king was startled for a moment, but collected himself immediately. "He suspects, but he is certain of nothing?"

"No, sire; but his suspicion amounts almost to certainty. Yesterday I was copying a dispatch which was to go that evening, and which was of the highest importance to your majesty, when I suddenly perceived Count Puebla standing beside me at my desk. He had entered my room very quietly, which showed that he had his suspicions, and was watching me. He snatched my copy from the desk and read it. 'For whom is this?' said he, in a threatening tone. I stammered forth some excuses; said that I intended writing a history, and that I took a copy of all dispatches for my work. He would not listen to me. 'You are a traitor!' said he, in a thundering voice. 'I have suspected you for some time; I am now convinced of your treachery. You shall have an examination tomorrow; for to-night you will remain a prisoner in your room.' He then locked my desk, put the key in his pocket, and, taking with him the dispatch and my copy, left the room. I heard him lock it and bolt my door. I was a prisoner."

"How did you get out?" said the king.

"By the window, sire. And I flew here to throw myself at your majesty's feet, and to beg for mercy and protection."

"I promised you protection and help in case of your detection—I will fulfil my promise. What are your wishes. Let us see if they can be realized."

"Will your majesty give me some sure place of refuge where Count Puebla's threats cannot harm me?"

"You will remain here in the dwelling of the castle-warder until a suitable residence can be found for you. What next? What plans have you made for the future?"

"I would humbly beseech your majesty to give me some position in your land worthy of my station, such as your highness promised me."

"You remember too many of my promises," said the king, shrugging his shoulders.

"Your majesty will not grant me the promised position?" said Count Weingarten, tremblingly.

"I remember no such promise," said Frederick. "Men of your stamp are paid, but not rewarded. I have made use of your treachery; but you are, nevertheless, in my eyes a traitor, and I will have none such in my service."

"Then I am lost!" said Weingarten. "My honor, my good name, my future are annihilated."

"Your honor has been weighed with gold," said the king, sternly, "and I think I have already paid more for it than it was worth. Your good name, it is true, will be from now changed into a bad one; and your mother will have to blush when she uses it. Therefore I advise you to let it go; to take another name; to begin a new existence, and to found a new future."

"A future without honor, without name, without position!" sighed Weingarten, despairingly.

"So are men!" said the king, softly; "insolent and stubborn when they think themselves secure; cowardly and uncertain when they are in danger. So you were rash enough to think that your treacherous deeds would always remain a secret? You did not think of a possible detection, or prepare yourself for it. In treading the road which you have trodden, every step should be considered. This, it seems to me, you have not done. You wish to enjoy the fruits of your treachery in perfect security; but you have not the courage to stand before the world as a traitor. Do away with this name, which will cause you many dangers and insults. Fly from this place, where you and your deeds are known. Under a different name look for an asylum in another part of my land. Money shall not fail you; and if what you have earned from me is not sufficient, turn to me, and I will lend you still more. I will not forget that to me your treachery has been of great use, and therefore I will not desert you, though I shall despise the traitor. And now, farewell! This is our last meeting. Call this afternoon upon my treasurer; he will pay you two hundred louis d'or. And now go." And with a scornful look at Weingarten's pale countenance, he turned to the window.

Weingarten hurried past the halls and chambers, and entered Rosa's room. She read in his pale, sad face that he had no good news to tell her.

"Has it all been in vain?" said she, breathlessly.

"In vain?" cried he, with a scornful smile. "No, not in vain. The king rewarded me well; much better than Judas Iscariot was rewarded. I have earned a large sum of money, and am still to receive a thousand crowns. Quiet yourself, Rosa; we will be very happy, for we will have money. Only I must ask if the proud daughter of the royal castle-warder will give her hand to a man who can offer her no name, no position. Rosa, I warn you, think well of what you do. You loved me because I was a count, and had position to offer you. From to-day, I have no position, no name, no honor, no family. Like Ahasuerus, I will wander wearily through the world, happy and thanking God if I can find a quiet spot where I am not known, and my name was never heard. There I will rest, and trust to chance for a name. Rosa, will you share with me this existence, without sunshine, without honor, without a name?"

She was trembling so, that she could barely speak.

"I have no choice," stammered she, at last; "I must follow you, for my honor demands that I should be your wife. I must go with you; fate wills it."

With a loud shriek she fainted by his side. Weingarten did not raise her; he glanced wildly at the pale, lifeless woman at his feet.

"We are both condemned," murmured he, "we have both lost our honor. And with this Cain's mark upon our foreheads we will wander wearily through the world." [*Footnote: Count Weingarten escaped from all his troubles happily. He married his sweetheart, the daughter of the castle-warder, and went to Altmark, where, under the name of Veis, he lived happily for many years.*]

The king, in the mean while, after Weingarten had left him, walked thoughtfully up and down his room. At times he raised his head and gazed with a proud, questioning glance at the sky. Great thoughts were at work within him. Now Frederick throws back his head proudly, and his eyes sparkle.

"The time has come," said he, in a loud, full voice. "The hour for delay is past; now the sword must decide between me and my enemies." He rang a bell hastily, and ordered a valet to send a courier at once to Berlin, to call General Winterfeldt, General Retzow, and also Marshal Schwerin, to Sans-Souci.

CHAPTER VIII
DECLARATION OF WAR

A few hours after the departure of the courier, the heavy movement of wheels in the court below announced to the king, who was standing impatiently at his window, the arrival of the expected generals. In the same moment, his chamberlain, opening wide the library door, ushered them into his presence.

"Ah!" said the king, welcoming them pleasantly, "I see I am not so entirely without friends as my enemies think. I have but to call, and Marshal Schwerin, that is, wisdom and victory, is at my side; and Generals Winterfeldt and Retzow, that is, youth and courage, boldness and bravery, are ready to give me all the assistance in their power. Sirs, I thank you for coming to me at once. Let us be seated; listen to what I have to say, and upon what earnest important subjects I wish your advice."

And in a few words the king first showed them the situation of Europe and of his own states, so as to prepare them for the more important subjects he had to introduce before them.

"You will now understand," said he, "why I was so willing to make this contract with England. I hoped thereby to gain Russia, who is allied to England, to my side. But these hopes have been destroyed. Russia, angry with Britain for having allied herself to Prussia, has broken her contract. Bestuchef, it is true, wavered for a moment between his love of English guineas and his hatred of me, but hate carried the day."

"But, sire," said Retzow, hastily, "if your majesty can succeed in making a reconciliation between France and England, you may become the ally of these two powerful nations. Then let Austria, Russia, and Saxony come upon us all at once, we can confront them."

"We can do that, I hope, even without the assistance of France," said the king, impetuously. "We must renounce all idea of help from France; she is allied to Austria. What Kaunitz commenced with his wisdom, Maria Theresa carried out with her flattery. All my enemies have determined to attack me at once. But I am ready for them, weapons in hand. I have been hard at work; all is arranged, every preparation for the march of our army is finished. And now I have called you together to counsel me as to where we can commence our attack advantageously."

Frederick stopped speaking, and gazed earnestly at his generals, endeavoring to divine their thoughts. Marshal Schwerin was looking silently before him; a dark cloud rested upon General Retzow's brow; but the young, handsome face of Winterfeldt was sparkling with delight at the thought of war.

"Well, marshal," said the king, impatiently, "what is your advice?"

"My advice, sire," said the old marshal, sighing; "I see my king surrounded by threatening and powerful foes; I see him alone in the midst of all these allied enemies. For England may, perchance, send us money, but she has no soldiers for us, and moreover, we must assist her to defend Hanover. I cannot counsel this war, for mighty enemies are around us, and Prussia stands alone."

"No," said Frederick, solemnly, "Prussia stands not alone!—a good cause and a good sword are her allies, and with them she will conquer. And now, General Retzow, let us have your opinion."

"I agree entirely with Marshal Schwerin," said Retzow. "Like him, I think Prussia should not venture into this strife, because she is too weak to withstand such powerful adversaries."

"You speak prudently," said Frederick, scornfully. "And now, Winterfeldt, are you also against this war?"

"No, sire," cried Winterfeldt, "I am for the attack, and never were circumstances more favorable than at present. Austria has as yet made no preparations for war; her armies are scattered, and her finances are in disorder; and now it will be an easy task to attack her and subdue her surprised army."

The king looked at him pleasantly, and turning to the other generals, said quietly.

"We must not be carried away by the brave daring of this youth; he is the youngest among us, and is, perhaps, misled by enthusiasm. But we old ones must reflect; and I wished to convince you that I had not failed to do this. But all has been in vain."

"Now is the time," said Winterfeldt, with sparkling eyes, "to convince the crippled, unwieldy Austrian eagle that the young eagle of Prussia has spread her wings, and that her claws are strong enough to grasp all her enemies and hurl them into an abyss."

"And if the young eagle, in spite of his daring, should have to succumb to the superiority of numbers," said Marshal Schwerin, sadly. "If the balls of his enemies should break his wings, thereby preventing his flight for the future? Were it not better to avoid this possibility, and not to allow the whole world to say that Prussia, out of love of conquest, began a fearful war, which she could have avoided?"

"There is no reason in this war," said General Retzow; "for, though Austria, Saxony, and Russia are not our friends, they have not shown as yet by any open act that they are our enemies; and though Austria's alliance with France surprised the world, so also did Prussia's alliance with England. Our soldiers will hardly know why they are going to battle, and they will be wanting in that inspiration which is necessary to excite an army to heroic deeds."

"Inspiration shall not be wanting, and my army as well as yourselves shall know the many causes we have for this war. The reasons I have given you as yet have not satisfied you? Well, then, I will give you others; and, by Heaven, you will be content with them! You think Austria's unkindly feelings to Prussia have not been shown by any overt act. I will now prove to you that she is on the point of acting." And Frederick, lifting up some papers from his desk, continued: "These papers will prove to you, what you seem determined not to believe, namely, that Saxony, Russia, and, France are prepared to attack Prussia with their combined forces, and to turn the kingdom of Prussia into a margraviate once more. These papers are authentic proofs of the dangers which hover over us. I will now inform you how I came by them, so that you may be convinced of their genuineness. For some time I have suspected that there was, amongst my enemies, an alliance against me, and that they had formed a contract in which they had sworn to do all in their power to destroy Prussia. I only needed to have my suspicions confirmed, and to have the proofs of this contract in my hands. There proofs were in the Saxon archives, and in the dispatches of the Austrian embassy. It was therefore necessary to get the key of these archives, and to have copies of these dispatches. I succeeded in doing both, Chance, or if you prefer it, a kind Providence, came to my aid. The Saxon chancellor, Reinitz, a former servant of General Winterfeldt, came from Dresden to Potsdam to look for Winterfeldt and to confide to him that a friend of his, Chancellor Minzel of Dresden, had informed him that the state papers interchanged between the court of Vienna and Dresden were kept in the Dresden archives, of which he had the key. Winterfeldt brought me this important message. Reinitz conducted the first negotiations with Menzel, which I then delivered into the hands of my ambassador in Dresden, Count Mattzahn. Menzel was poor and covetous. He was therefore easily to be bribed. For three years

Mattzahn has received copies of every dispatch that passed between the three courts. I am quite as well informed of all negotiations between Austria and France, for the secretary of the Austrian legation of this place, a Count Weingarten, gave me, for promises and gold, copies of all dispatches that came from Vienna and were forwarded to France. You see the corruption of man has borne me good fruit, and that gold is a magic wand which reveals all secrets. And now let us cast a hasty glance over these papers which I have obtained by the aid of treachery and bribery."

He took one of the papers and spread it before the astonished generals. "You see here," he continued, "a sample of all other negotiations. It is a copy of a share contract which the courts of Vienna and Dresden formed in 1745. They then regarded the decline of Prussia as so sure an occurrence that they had already divided amongst themselves the different parts of my land. Russia soon affixed her name also to this contract, and here in this document you will see that these three powers have sworn to attack Prussia at the same moment, and that for this conquest, each one of the named courts was to furnish sixty thousand men."

While the generals were engaged in reading these papers, the king leaned back in his arm-chair, gazing keenly at Retzow and Schwerin. He smiled gayly as he saw Schwerin pressing his lips tightly together, and trying in vain to suppress a cry of rage, and Retzow clinching his fists vehemently.

When the papers had been read, and Schwerin was preparing to speak, the king, with his head thrown proudly back, and gazing earnestly at his listeners, interrupted him, saying:

"Now, sirs, perhaps you see the dangers by which we are surrounded. Under the circumstances, I owe it to myself, to my honor, and to the security of my land, to attack Austria and Saxony, and so to nip their abominable designs in me bud, before their allies are ready to give them any assistance. I am prepared, and the only question to be answered before setting our army in motion, is where to commence the attack to our advantage? For the deciding of this question, I have called you together. I have finished and now, Marshal Schwerin, it is your turn."

The old gray warrior arose. It may be that he was convinced by the powerful proofs and words of the king, or that knowing that his will was law it were vain to oppose him, but he was now as strongly for war as the king or Winterfeldt.

"If there is to be war," said he, enthusiastically, "let us start to-morrow, take Saxony, and, in that land of corn, build magazines for the holding of our provisions, so as to secure a way for our future operations in Bohemia."

"Ah! now I recognize my old Schwerin," said the king, gayly pressing the marshal's hand. "No more delay! 'To anticipate' is my motto, and shall, God willing, be Prussia's in future."

"And our army," said Winterfeldt, with sparkling eyes, "has been accustomed, for hundreds of years, not only to defend themselves, but also to attack. Ah, at last it is to be granted us to fight our arch-enemies in open field, mischief-making Austria, intriguing Saxony, barbarous Russia, and finally lying, luxurious France, and to convince them that, though we do not fear their anger, we share their hatred with our whole hearts."

"And you, Retzow," said the king, sternly, turning to the general, who was sitting silently with downcast head; "do your views coincide with Schwerin's? Or do you still think it were better to wait?"

"Yes, sire," said Retzow, sadly; "I think delay, under the present threatening circumstances, would be the wisest course; I—"

He was interrupted by the entrance of a valet, who approached the king, and whispered a few words to him.

Frederick turned smilingly to the generals. "The princes, my brothers, have arrived," said he; "they were to be here at this hour to hear the result of our consultation. And, it strikes me, they arrive at the right moment. The princes may enter."

CHAPTER IX
THE KING AND HIS BROTHERS

The door was thrown open and the princes entered. First came the Prince of Prussia, whose pale, dejected countenance was to-day paler and sadder than usual. Then Prince Henry, whose quick bright eyes were fixed inquiringly on General Retzow. The general shrugged his shoulders, and shook his head. Prince Henry must have understood these movements, for his brow became clouded, and a deep red suffused his countenance. The king, who had seen this, laughed mockingly, and let the princes approach very close to him, before addressing them.

"Sirs," said he, "I have called you here, because I have some important news to communicate. The days of peace are over and war is at hand!"

"War! and with whom?" said the Prince of Prussia, earnestly. "War with our enemies!" cried the king. "War with those who have sworn Prussia's destruction. War with Austria, France, Saxony, and Russia!"

"That is impossible, my brother," cried the prince, angrily. "You cannot dream of warring against such powerful nations. You cannot believe in the possibility of victory. Powerful and mighty as your spirit is it will have to succumb before the tremendous force opposed to it. Oh! my brother! my king! be merciful to yourself, to us, to our country. Do not desire the impossible! Do not venture into the stormy sea of war, to fight with your frail barks against the powerful men of war that your enemies, will direct against you. We cannot be victorious! Preserve to your country your own precious life, and that of her brave sons."

The king's eyes burned with anger; they were fixed with an expression of deep hatred upon the prince.

"Truly, my brother," said he, in a cold, cutting tone, "fear has made you eloquent. You speak as if inspired."

A groan escaped the prince, and he laid his hand unwittingly upon his sword. He was deadly pale, and his lips trembled so violently, that he could scarcely speak.

"Fear!" said he, slowly. "That is an accusation which none but the king would dare to bring against me, and of which I will clear myself, if it comes to this unhappy war which your majesty proposes, and which I now protest against, in the name of my rights, my children, and my country."

"And I," said Prince Henry, earnestly — "I also protest against this war! Have pity on us, my king. Much as I thirst for renown and glory, often as I have prayed to God to grant me an occasion to distinguish myself, I now swear to subdue forever this craving for renown, if it can only be obtained at the price of this frightful, useless war. You stand alone! Without allies, it is impossible to conquer. Why, then, brave certain ruin and destruction?"

The king's countenance was frightful to look at; his eyes were flashing with rage, and his voice was like thunder, it was so loud and threatening.

"Enough of this!" said he; "you were called here, not to advise, but to receive my commands. The brother has heard you patiently, but now the King of Prussia stands before you, and demands of you obedience and submission. We are going to battle; this is settled; and your complaints and fears will not alter my determination But all those who fear to follow me on the battle-field, have my permission to remain at home, and pass their time in love idyls. Who, amongst you all, prefers this? Let him speak, and he shall follow his own inclinations."

"None of us could do that," said Prince Henry, passionately "If the King of Prussia calls his soldiers, they will all come and follow their chieftain joyfully, though they are marching to certain death. I have already given you my personal opinion; it now rests with me to obey you, as a soldier, as a subject. This I will do joyfully, without complaining."

"I also," said Prince Augustus William, earnestly. "Like my brother, I will know how to subdue my own opinions and fears, and to follow in silent obedience my king and my chieftain."

The king threw a glance of hatred upon the pale, disturbed countenance of the prince.

"You will go where I command you," said he, sharply; and not giving the prince time to answer, he turned abruptly to Marshal Schwerin.

"Well, marshal, do you wish for a furlough, during this war? You heard me say I would refuse it to no one."

"I demand nothing of your majesty, but to take part in the first battle against your enemies. I do not ask who they are. The hour for consultation is past: it is now time to act. Let us to work, and that right quickly."

"Yes, to battle, sire," cried Retzow, earnestly. "As soon as your majesty has said that this war is irrevocable, your soldiers must have no further doubts, and they will follow you joyfully, to conquer or to die."

"And you, Winterfeldt," said the king, taking his favorite's hand tenderly; "have you nothing to say? Or have the Prince of Prussia's fears infected you, and made of you a coward?"

"Ah, no! sire," said Winterfeldt, pressing the king's hand to his breast; "how could my courage fail, when it is Prussia's hero king that leads to battle? How can I be otherwise than joyous and confident of victory, when Frederick calls us to fight against his wicked and arrogant enemies? No! I have no fears; God and the true cause is on our side."

Prince Henry approached nearer to the king, and looking at him proudly, he said:

"Sire, you asked General Winterfeldt if he shared the Prince of Prussia's fears. He says no; but I will beg your majesty to remember, that I share entirely the sentiments of my dear and noble brother."

As he finished, he threw an angry look at General Winterfeldt. The latter commenced a fierce rejoinder, but was stopped by the king. "Be still, Winterfeldt," he said; "war has as yet not been declared, and till then, let there at least be peace in my own house." Then approaching Prince Henry, and laying his hand on his shoulder, he said kindly: "We will not exasperate each other, my brother. You have a noble, generous soul, and no one would dare to doubt your courage. It grieves me that you do not share my views as to the necessity of this war, but I know that you will be a firm, helpful friend, and share with me my dangers, my burdens, and if God wills it, also my victory."

"Not I alone will do this," cried Prince Henry, "but also my brother, Augustus William, the Prince of Prussia, whose heart is not less brave, whose courage—"

"Hush, Henry! I pray you," said the Prince of Prussia, sadly; "speak not of my courage. By defending it, it would seem that it had been doubted, and that is a humiliation which I would stand from no one"

The king appeared not to have heard these words. He took some papers from the table by which he was standing, and said:

"All that remains to be told you now, is that I agree with Marshal Schwerin. We will commence the attack in Saxony. To Saxony, then, gentlemen! But, until the day before the attack, let us keep even the question of war a secret."

Then, with the paper under his arm, he passed through the saloon and entered his library.

There was a long pause after he left. The Prince of Prussia, exhausted by the storm which had swept over his soul, had withdrawn to one of the windows, where he was hid from view by the heavy satin damask curtains.

Prince Henry, standing alone in the middle of the room, gazed after his brother, and a deep sigh escaped him. Then turning to Retzow, he said:

"You would not, then, fulfil my brother's and my own wishes?"

"I did all that was in my power, prince," said the general, sighing. "Your highness did not wish this war to take place; you desired me, if the king asked for my advice, to tell him that we were too weak, and should therefore keep the peace. Well, I said this, not only because you desired it, but because it was also my own opinion. But the king's will was unalterable. He has meditated this war for years. Years ago, with Winterfeldt's aid, he drew all the plans and made every other arrangement."

"Winterfeldt!" murmured the prince to himself, "yes, Winterfeldt is the fiend whose whispers have misled the king. We suspected this long ago, but we had to bear it in silence, for we could not prevent it."

And giving his passionate nature full play, he approached General Winterfeldt, who was whispering to Marshal Schwerin.

"You can rejoice, general," said the prince, "for now you can take your private revenge on the Empress of Russia."

Winterfeldt encountered the prince's angry glance with a quiet, cheerful look.

"Your highness does me too much honor in thinking that a poor soldier, such as I am, could be at enmity with a royal empress. What could this Russian empress have done to me, that could call for revenge on my part?"

"What has she done to you?" said the prince, with a mocking smile. "Two things, which man finds hardest to forgive! She outwitted you, and took your riches from you. Ah! general, I fear this war will be in vain, and that you will not be able to take your wife's jewels from St. Petersburg, where the empress retains them."

Winterfeldt subdued his anger, and replied: "You have related us a beautiful fairy tale, prince, a tale from the Arabian Nights, in which there is a talk of jewels and glorious treasures, only that in this tale, instead of the usual dragon, an empress guards them. I acknowledge that I do not understand your highness."

"But I understand you perfectly, general. I know your ambitious and proud plans. You wish to make your name renowned. General, I consider you are much in fault as to this war. You were the king's confidant—you had your spies everywhere, who, for heavy rewards, imparted to you the news by which you stimulated the king."

"If in your eyes," said Winterfeldt, proudly, "it is wrong to spend your gold to find out the intrigues of your own, your king's, and your country's enemies, I acknowledge that I am in fault, and deserve to be punished. Yes, everywhere I have had my spies, and thanks to them, the king knows Saxony's, Austria's, and Russia's intentions. I paid these spies with my own gold. Your highness may thus perceive that I am not entirely dependent on those jewels of my wife which are said to be in the Empress of Russia's possession."

At this moment the Prince of Prussia, who had been a silent witness to this scene, approached General Winterfeldt.

"General," said he, in a loud, solemn voice, "you are the cause of this unfortunate war which will soon devastate our poor land. The responsibility falls upon your head, and woe to you if this war, caused by your ambition, should be the ruin of our beloved country! I would, if there were no punishment for you on earth, accuse you before the throne of God, and the blood of the slaughtered sons of my country, the blood of my future subjects, would cry to Heaven for revenge! Woe to you it this war should be the ruin of Prussia!" repeated Prince Henry. "I could never forgive that; I would hold your ambition responsible for it, for you have access to the king's heart, and instead of dissipating his distrust against these foreign nations, you have endeavored to nourish it—instead of softening the king's anger, you have given it fresh food."

"What I have done," cried Winterfeldt, solemnly raising his right hand heavenward—"what I have done was done from a feeling of duty, from love of my country, and from a firm, unshaken trust in my king's star, which cannot fade, but must become ever more and more resplendent! May God punish me if I have acted from other and less noble motives!"

"Yes, may God punish you—may He not revenge your crime upon our poor country!" said Prince Augustus William. "I have said my last upon this sad subject. From now on, my private opinions are subdued—I but obey the king's commands. What he requires of me shall be done—where he sends me I will go, without questioning or considering, but quietly and obediently, as it becomes a true soldier. I hope that you, my brother, Marshal Schwerin, and General Retzow, will follow my example. The king has commanded, we have but to obey cheerfully."

Then, arm in arm, the princes left the audience-room and returned to Berlin.

CHAPTER X
THE LAUREL-BRANCH

While this last scene was passing in the audience-room, the king had retired to his study, and was walking up and down in deep thought. His countenance was stern and sorrowful—a dark cloud was upon his brow—his lips were tightly pressed together—powerful emotions were disturbing his whole being. He stopped suddenly, and raising his head proudly, seemed to be listening to the thoughts and suggestions of his soul.

"Yes," said he, "these were his very words: 'I protest against this war in the name of my rights, my children, and my country!' Ah, it is a pleasant thought to him that he is to be heir to my throne. He imagines that he has rights beyond those that I grant him, and that he can protest against an action of mine! He is a rebel, a traitor. He dares to think of the time when I will be gone—of the time when he or his children will wear this crown! I feel that I hate him as my father hated me because I was his heir, and because the sight of me always reminded him of his death! Yes, I hate him! The effeminate boy will disturb the great work which I am endeavoring to perform. Under his weak hands, this Prussia, which I would make great and powerful, will fail to pieces, and all my battles and conquests will be in vain. He will not know how to make use of them. I will make of my Prussia a mighty and much-feared nation. And if I succeed, by giving up my every thought to this one object, then my brother will come and destroy this work which has cost me such pain and trouble. Prussia needs a strong, active king, not an effeminate boy who passes his life in sighing for his lost love and in grumbling at fate for making him the son of a king. Yes, I feel that I hate him, for I foresee that he will be the destroyer of my great work. But no, no—I do him wrong," said the king, "and my suspicious heart sees, perhaps, things that are not. Ah, has it gone so far? Must I, also, pay the tribute which princes give for their pitiful splendor? I suspect the heir to my throne, and see in him a secret enemy! Mistrust has already thrown her shadow upon my soul, and made it dark and troubled. Ah, there will come a cold and dreary night for me, when I shall stand alone in the midst of all my glory!"

His head fell upon his breast, and he remained silent and immovable.

"And am I not alone, now?" said he, and in his voice there was a soft and sorrowful sound. "My brothers are against me, because they do not understand me; my sisters fear me, and, because this war will disturb their peace and comfort, will hate me. My mother's heart has cooled toward me, because I will not be influenced by her; and Elizabeth Christine, whom the world calls my wife, weeps in solitude over the heavy chains which bind her. Not one of them loves me!—not one believes in me, and in my future!"

The king, given up to these melancholy thoughts, did not hear a knock at his door; it was now repeated, and so loudly, that he could not but hear it. He hastened to the door and opened it. Winterfeldt was there, with a sealed paper in his hand, which he gave to the king, begging him at the same time to excuse this interruption.

"It is the best thing you could have done," said the king, entering his room, and signing to the general to follow him. "I was in bad company, with my own sorrowful thoughts, and it is good that you came to dissipate them."

"This letter will know well how to do that," said Winterfeldt handing him the packet; "a courier brought it to me from Berlin."

"Letters from my sister Wilhelmina, from Italy," said the king, joyfully breaking the seal, and unfolding the papers.

There were several sheets of paper closely written, and between them lay a small, white packet. The king kept the latter in his hand, and commenced reading eagerly. As he read, the dark, stern expression gradually left his countenance. His brow was smooth and calm, and a soft, beautiful smile played about his lips. He finished the letter, and throwing it hastily aside, tore open the package. In it was a laurel-branch, covered with beautiful leaves, which looked as bright and green as if they had just been cut. The king raised it, and looked at it tenderly. "Ah, my friend," said he, with a beaming smile, "see how kind Providence is to me! On this painful day she sends me a glorious token, a laurel-branch. My sister gathered it for me on my birthday. Do you know where, my friend? Bow your head, be all attention; for know that it is a branch from the laurel-tree that grows upon Virgil's grave! Ah, my friend, it seems to me as if the great and glorious spirits of the olden ages were greeting me with this laurel which came from the grave of one of their greatest poets. My sister sends it to me, accompanied by some beautiful verses of her own. An old fable says that these laurels grew spontaneously upon Virgil's grave, and that they are indestructible. May this be a blessed omen for me! I greet you, Virgil's holy shadow! I bow down before you, and kiss in all humility your ashes, which have been turned into laurels!"

Thus speaking, the king bowed his head, and pressed a fervent kiss upon the laurel. He then handed it to Winterfeldt. "Do likewise, my friend," said he; "your lips are worthy to touch this holy branch, to inhale the odor of these leaves which grew upon Virgil's grave. Kiss this branch—and now let us swear to become worthy of this kiss; swear that in this war, which will soon begin, laurels shall either rest upon our brows or upon our graves!"

Winterfeldt having sworn, repeated these words after him, "Amen!" said the king; "God and Virgil have heard us."

CHAPTER XI
THE BALL AT COUNT BRUHL'S

Count Bruhl, first minister to the King of Saxony, gave to-day a magnificent fete in his palace, in honor of his wife, whose birthday it was. The feast was to be honored by the presence of the King of Poland, the Prince Elector of Saxony, Augustus III., and Maria Josephine, his wife. This was a favor which the proud queen granted to her favorite for the first time. For she who had instituted there the stern Spanish etiquette to which she had been accustomed at the court of her father, Joseph I., had never taken a meal at the table of one of her subjects; so holy did she consider her royal person, that the ambassadors of foreign powers were not permitted to sit at the same table with her. Therefore, at every feast at the court of Dresden, there was a small table set apart for the royal family, and only the prime minister, Count Bruhl, was deserving of the honor to eat with the king and queen. This was a custom which pleased no one so well as the count himself, for it insured him from the danger that some one might approach the royal pair, and inform them of some occurrence of which the count wished them to remain in ignorance.

There were many slanderers in this wretched kingdom—many who were envious of the count's high position—many who dared to believe that the minister employed the king's favor for his own good, and not for that of his country. They said that he alone lived luxuriously in this miserable land, while the people hungered; that he spent every year over a million of thalers. They declared that he had not less than five millions now lying in the banks of Rotterdam, Venice, and Marseilles; others said that he had funds to the amount of seven millions. One of these calumniators might possibly approach the king's table and whisper into the royal ear his wicked slanders; one of these evil-doers might even have the audacity to make his unrighteous complaints to the queen. This it was that caused Count Bruhl to tremble; this it was that robbed him of sleep at night, of peace by day, this fear of a possible disgrace.

He was well acquainted with the history of Count Lerma, minister to King Philip IV. of Spain. Lerma was also the ruler of a king, and reigned over Spain, as Bruhl over Saxony. All had succumbed to his power and influence, even the royal family trembled when he frowned, and felt themselves honored by his smile. What was it that caused the ruin of this all-powerful, irreproachable favorite? A little note which King Philip found between his napkin one day, upon which was this address: "To Philip IV., once King of Spain, and Master of both the Indies, but now in the service of Count Lerma!" This it was that caused the count's ruin; Philip was enraged by this note, and the powerful favorite fell into disgrace.

Count Bruhl knew this history, and was on his guard. He knew that even the air which he breathed was poisoned by the malice of his enemies; that those who paused in the streets to greet him reverentially when he passed in his gilded carriage, cursed him in their inmost hearts; that those friends who pressed his hand and sung songs in his praise, would become his bitterest enemies so soon as he ceased paying for their friendship with position, with pensions, with honors, and with orders. He spent hundreds of thousands yearly to gain friends and admirers, but still he was in constant fear that some enemy would undermine him. This had indeed once happened. During the time that the king's favor was shared equally with Count Bruhl, Count Sulkovsky, and Count Hennicke, whilst playing cards, a piece of gold was given to the king, upon which was represented the crown of Poland, resting upon the shoulders of three men, with the following inscription: "There are three of us, two pages and one lackey!" The King of Poland was as much enraged by this satirical piece of gold as was the King of Spain by his satirical note. But Count Bruhl succeeded in turning the king's anger upon the two other shoulder-bearers of his crown. Counts Sulkovsky and Hennicke fell into disgrace, and were banished from the court; Count Bruhl remained, and reigned as absolute master over Poland and Saxony!

But reigning, he still trembled, and therefore he favored the queen's fancy for the strictest etiquette; therefore, no one but Count Bruhl was to eat at the royal table; he himself took their napkins from their plates and handed them to the royal couple; no one was to approach the sovereigns who was not introduced by the prime minister, who was at once master of ceremonies, field-marshal, and grand chamberlain, and received for each of these different posts a truly royal salary. Etiquette and the fears of the powerful favorite kept the royal pair almost prisoners.

But for to-day etiquette was to be done away with; the crowned heads were to be gracious, so as to lend a new glory to their favorite's house. To-day the count was fearless, for there was no danger of a traitor being among his guests. His wife and himself had drawn up the list of invitations. But still, as there might possibly be those among them who hated the count, and would very gladly injure him, he had ordered some of the best paid of his friends to watch all suspicious characters, not to leave them alone for a moment, and not to overlook a single word of theirs. Of course, it was understood that the count and his wife must remain continually at the side of the king and queen, that all who wished to speak to them must first be introduced by the host or hostess.

The count was perfectly secure to-day, and therefore gay and happy. He had been looking at the different arrangements for this feast, and he saw with delight that they were such as to do honor to his house. It was, to be a summer festival: the entire palace had been turned into a greenhouse, that served only for an entrance to the actual scene of festivities. This was the immense garden. In the midst of the rarest and most beautiful groups of flowers, immense tents were raised; they were of rich, heavy silk, and were festooned at the sides with golden cords and tassels. Apart from these was a smaller one, which outshone them all in magnificence. The roof of this tent rested upon eight pillars of gold; it was composed of a dark-red velvet, over which a slight gauze, worked with gold and silver stars, was gracefully arranged. Upon the table below this canopy, which rested upon a rich Turkish carpet, there was a heavy service of gold, and the most exquisite Venetian glass; the immense pyramid in the middle of the table was a master-work of Benevenuto Cellini, for which the count had paid in Rome one hundred thousand thalers. There were but seven seats, for no one was to eat at this table but the royal pair, the prince-elector and his wife, the Prince Xavier, and the Count and Countess Bruhl. This was a new triumph that the count had prepared for himself; he wished his guests to see the exclusive royal position he occupied. And no one could remain in ignorance of this triumph, for from every part of the garden the royal tent could be seen, being erected upon a slight eminence. It was like a scene from fairyland. There were rushing cascades, beautiful marble statues, arbors and bowers, in which were birds of every color from every clime. Behind a group of trees was a lofty structure of the purest marble, a shell, borne aloft by gigantic Tritons and mermaids, in which there was room for fifty musicians, who were to fill the air with sweet sounds, and never to become so loud as to weary the ear or disturb conversation. If the tents, the rushing cascades, the rare flowers, the many colored birds, were a beautiful sight by daylight, how much more entrancing it would be at night, when illuminated by thousands of brilliant lamps!

The count, having taken a last look at the arrangements and seen that they were perfect, now retired to his rooms, and there, with the aid of his twelve valets, he commenced his toilet. The countess had already been in the hands of her Parisian coiffeur for some hours.

The count wore a suit of blue velvet. The price of embroidery in silver and pearls on his coat would have furnished hundreds of wretched, starving families with bread. His diamond shoe-buckles would almost have sufficed to pay the army, which had gone unpaid for months. When his toilet was finished, he entered his study to devote a few moments, at least, to his public duties, and to read those letters which to-day's post had brought him from all parts of the world, and which his secretary was accustomed to place in his study at this hour. He took a letter, broke the seal hastily, and skimming over it quickly, threw it aside and opened another, to read anew the complaints, the prayers, the flatteries, the assurances of love, of his correspondents. But none of them were calculated to compel the minister's attention. He had long ago hardened his heart against prayers and complaints; as for flattery, he well knew that he had to pay for it with pensions, with position, with titles, with orders, etc., etc. But it seemed as if the letters were not all of the usual sort, for the expression of indifference which had rested upon his countenance while reading the others, had vanished and given place to one of a very different character. This letter was from Flemming, the Saxon ambassador in Berlin, and contained strange, wild rumors. The King of Prussia, it seemed, had left Berlin the day before, with all the princes and his staff officers, and no one knew exactly where he was going! Rumor said, though, that he and his army were marching toward Saxony! After reading this, Count Bruhl broke out into a loud laugh.

"Well," said he, "it must be granted that this little poet-king, Frederick, has the art of telling the most delightful fairy-tales to his subjects, and of investing every action of his with the greatest importance. Ah, Margrave of Brandenburg! we will soon be in a condition to take your usurped crown from your head. Parade as much as you like—make the world believe in you and your absurd manoeuvres—the day will soon come when she will but see in you a poor knight with naught but his title of marquis." With a triumphant smile he threw down the letter and grasped the next. "Another from Flemming?" said he. "Why, truly, the good count is becoming fond of writing. Ah," said he, after reading it carelessly, "more warnings! He declares that the King of Prussia intends attacking Saxony—that he is now already at our borders. He then adds, that the king is aware of the contract which we and our friends have signed, swearing to attack Prussia simultaneously. Well, my good Flemming, there is not much wisdom needed to tell me that if the king knows of our contract, he will be all the more on his guard, and will make preparations to defend himself; for he would not be so foolhardy as to attempt to attack our three united armies. No, no. Our regiments can remain quietly in Poland, the seventeen thousand men here will answer all purposes."

"There is but one more of these begging letters," said he, opening it, but throwing it aside without reading it. Out of it fell a folded piece of paper.

"Why," said the count, taking it up, "there are verses. Has Flemming's fear of the Prussian king made a poet of him?" He opened it and read aloud:

"'A piece of poetry which a friend, Baron Pollnitz, gave me yesterday. The author is the King of Prussia.'"

"Well," said the count, laughing, "a piece of poetry about me—the king does me great honor. Let us see; perhaps these verses can be read at the table to-day, and cause some amusement. 'Ode to Count Bruhl,' with this inscription: 'il ne faut pas s'inquieter de l'avsnir.' That is a wise philosophical sentence, which nevertheless did not spring from the brain of his Prussian majesty. And now for the verses." And straightening the paper before him, he commenced.

> *"Esclave malheureux de la haute fortune,*
>
> *D'un roi trop indolent souverain absolu,*
>
> *Surcharge de travaux dont le soin L'importune.*
>
> *Bruhl, quitte des grandeurs L'embarras superflu.*
>
> *Au sein de ton opulence*
>
> *Je vois le Dieu des ennuis,*
>
> *Et dans ta magnificence*
>
> *Le repos fait tes units.*

> *"Descend de ce palais dont le superbe faite*
>
> *Domine sur la Saxe, s'elevent aux cieux.*
>
> *D'ou ton esprit craintif conjure la tempete*
>
> *Que souleve ala cour un peuple d'envieux:*
>
> *Vois cette grandeur fragile*
>
> *Et cesse enfin d'admirer*
>
> *L'eclat pompeux d'une ville*
>
> *Ou tout feint de t'adorer."*

The count's voice had at first been loud, pathetic, and slightly ironical, but it became gradually lower, and sank at last almost to a whisper. A deep, angry red suffused his face, as he read on. Again his voice became louder as he read the last two verses:

"Connaissez la Fortune inconstante et legere;

La perfide se plait aux plus cruels revers,

On la voit, abuber le sage, le vulgaire,

Jouer insolemment tout ce faible univers;

Aujourd'hui c'est sur ma tete

Qu'elle repand des faveurs,

Des demain elle s'apprete

A les emporter ailleurs."

"Fixe-t-elle sur moi sa bizarre inconstance,

Mon concur lui saura gre' du bien qu'elle me fait

Veut'elle en d'autres lieux marquer sa bienvellance,

Je lui remets ses dons sans chagrin, sans regret.

Plein d'une vertu plus forte

J'epouse la pauvrete'

Si pour dot elle m'apporte

L'honneur et la probite'"

[Footnote: ODE TO COUNT BRUHL. Inscription. —*"It is not necessary to make ourselves uneasy about the future."*

"High Destiny's unhappy slave,

Absolute lord of too indolent a king,

Oppressed with work whose care importunes him—

Bruhl, leave the useless perplexities of grandeur.

In the bosom of thine opulence

I see the God of the wearied ones,

And in thy magnificence

Repose makes thy nights."

"Descend from this palace, whose haughty dome

Towering o'er Saxony, rises to the skies;

In which thy fearful mind confines the tempest.

Which agitates at the court, a nation of enviers.

Look at this fragile grandeur,

And cease at last to admire

The pompous shining of a city

Where all feign to adore thee."

"Know that Fortune is light and inconstant;

A deceiver who delights

in cruel reverses;

She is seen to abuse the wise man, the vulgar

Insolently playing with all this weak universe.

To-day it is on my head

That she lets her favors fall,

By to-morrow she will be prepared

To carry them elsewhere."

"Does she fix on me her wayward fickleness,

My heart will be grateful for the good she does me;

Does she wish to show elsewhere her benevolence,

I give her back her gifts without pain—without regret.

Filled with strongest virtue,

I will espouse Poverty,

If for dower she brings me

Honor and probity."]

The paper fell from the count's hand and he looked at it thoughtfully. An expression of deep emotion rested upon his countenance, which, in spite of his fifty years, could still be called handsome—as he repeated in a low, trembling voice:

"J'epouse la pauvrete, Si pour dot elle m'apporte L'honneur et la probite."

The sun coming through the window rested upon his tall form, causing the many jewels upon his garments to sparkle like stars on the blue background, enveloping him in a sort of glory. He had repeated for the third time, "J'epouse la pauvrete," when the door leading to his wife's apartments was opened, and the countess entered in the full splendor of her queenly toilet, sparkling with jewels. The count was startled by her entrance, but he now broke out into a loud, mocking laugh.

"Truly, countess," said he, "you could not have found a better moment to interrupt me. For the last half hour my thoughts have been given up to sentiment. Wonderful dreams have been chasing each other through my brain. But you have again shown yourself my good angel, Antonia, by dissipating these painful thoughts." He pressed a fervent kiss upon her hand, then looking at her with a beaming countenance, he said:

"How beautiful you are, Antonia; you must have found that mysterious river which, if bathed in, insures perpetual youth and beauty."

"Ah!" said the countess, smiling, "all know that no one can flatter so exquisitely as Count Bruhl."

"But I am not always paid with the same coin, Antonia," said the count, earnestly. "Look at this poem, that the King of Prussia has written of me. Truly, there is no flattery in it."

While reading, the countess's countenance was perfectly clear; not the slightest cloud was to be seen upon her brow.

"Do you not think it a good poem?" said she, indifferently.

"Well," said he, "I must acknowledge that there was a certain fire in it that touched my heart."

"I find it stupid," said she, sternly. "There is but one thing in it that pleases me, and that is the title-'il ne faut pas s'inquieter de l'avenir.' The little King of Prussia has done well to choose this for his motto, for without it, it strikes me, his peace would be forever gone, for his future will surely be a humiliating one."

The count laughed.

"How true that is!" said he "and a just answer to his stupid poem. Speak of something else."

He tore the paper into small pieces, which, with a graceful bow, he laid at the feet of the countess.

"A small sacrifice," said he, "which I bring to my goddess. Tread upon it, and destroy the king's words with your fairy foot." The countess obeyed him, laughingly.

"But now, count," said she, "we will, for a moment, speak of graver things. I have received letters from Loudon-from our son. Poor Henry is in despair, and he has requested me to intercede for him. You were always very stern with him, my friend, therefore he fears your anger, now that he has been a little imprudent."

"Well, what is it?" said the count; "I hope it is no duel, for that would make me extremely angry."

"It is nothing of that kind. His imprudence is of another sort, He is in want of money."

"Money!" said the count, in amazement; "why, barely a month ago, I sent him six hundred thousand thalers. That, and what he took with him, three months ago, is quite a large sum, for it amounts to more than a million of thalers."

"But, my dear husband, in England every thing is so dear! and there, to move amongst and impress those rich lords, he must really have more. It seems that our Charles Joseph has fallen in love with a lady whom all Loudon worships for her surpassing beauty. But she, having a cold heart, will listen to no one. She laughs at those who flatter her, and will receive no presents. She seemed an invincible fortress, but our son, thanks to stratagem, has taken it."

"I am curious to know how," said the count, laughing.

"He played a game of ecarte with her. He played for notes to the amount of ten pounds, and, at first, Charles won, much to the displeasure of the proud lady, who did not relish being beaten, even in a game of cards. Charles, perceiving this, played badly. The lady won from him eighty thousand pounds."

"Eighty thousand pounds," cried the count, "why, that is a half a million of thalers!"

"And do you mean to say," said the countess, angrily, "that that is too much to gain the favor of a beautiful lady?"

"No! it is not too much; but it is certainly enough. I hope, at least, it was not in vain."

"No, no! and Loudon is now raving about the intellectual, genial and generous son of Count Bruhl. I trust, count, that you instantly sent him a check."

"Yes," said the count, shrugging his shoulders. "But, countess, if the king were to hear this story, it would cause much evil; for you know that he believes in economy; luckily for me, he believes me to be an economical man. Those enemies who would not dare to accuse us, would have no fears of saying evil of our son; he will certainly hear this eighty-thousand-pound story."

"We will tell him ourselves, but say that the story is much exaggerated."

"What a wonderful woman you are, Antonia!" said her husband; "your counsel is wise; we will follow it."

At this moment a slight knocking was heard at the door, and the secretary entered with a sealed letter.

"A courier from Torgau just arrived with this from the commandant." The count's brow became clouded.

"Business! forever business!" said he. "How dared you annoy me with this, upon the birthday of my wife?"

"Pardon, your excellency; but the courier brought with this packet such strange news, that I ventured to disturb you, to communicate—"

The beating of drums and the thunder of cannon interrupted him.

"The king and queen are now entering their carriage," cried the count. "No more business to-day, my friend. It will keep till tomorrow. Come, Antonia, we must welcome their majesties." And taking his wife's hand, he passed out of the study.

CHAPTER XII
THE INTERRUPTED FEAST

As the Count Bruhl and his wife entered the saloon, it almost seemed as if they were the royal couple for whom all this company was waiting. Every one of any rank or position in Dresden was present. There were to be seen the gold and silver embroidered uniforms of generals and ambassadors; jewelled stars were sparkling upon many breasts; the proudest, loveliest women of the court, bearing the noblest Saxon names, were there, accompanied by princes, counts, dukes, and barons, and one and all were bowing reverentially to the count and his wife. And now, at a sign from the grand chamberlain, the pages of the countess, clothed in garments embroidered with silver and pearls, approached to carry her train; beside them were the count's officers, followed by all the noble guests. Thus they passed through the third room, where the servants of the house, numbering upward of two hundred, were placed in military order, and then on until they came to the grand entrance, which had been turned into a floral temple.

The royal equipage was at the gate; the host and hostess advanced to welcome the king and queen, whose arrival had been announced by the roar of cannon.

The king passed through the beautiful avenue, and greeted the company placed on either side of him, gayly. The queen, sparkling with diamonds, forcing herself also to smile, was at his side; and as their majesties passed on, saying here and there a kind, merry word, it seemed as if the sun had just risen over all these noble, rich, and powerful guests. This was reflected upon every countenance. The gods had demanded from Olympus to favor these mortals with their presence, and to enjoy themselves among them. And truly, even a king might spend some happy hours in this delightful garden.

The air was so soft and mild, so sweet from the odor of many flowers; the rustling of the trees was accompanied by soft whispers of music that seemed floating like angels' wings upon the air. Every countenance was sparkling with happiness and content, and the king could but take the flattering unction to his soul that all his subjects were equally as happy as the elite by which he was surrounded.

Pleased with this thought and delighted with all the arrangements for the fete, the king gave himself up to an enjoyment which, though somewhat clouding his character as a deity, was immensely gratifying to him.

He abandoned himself to the delights of the table! He devoured with a sort of amiable astonishment the rare and choice dishes which, even to his experienced and pampered palate, appeared unfathomable mysteries; luxuries had been procured, not only from Loudon and Paris, but from every part of the world. He delighted himself with the gold and purple wines, whose vintage was unknown to him, and whose odor intoxicated him more than the perfume of flowers. He requested the count to give the name and history of all these wines.

The count obeyed in that shy, reverential manner in which he was accustomed to speak. He charmed him by relating the many difficulties he had overcome to obtain this wine from the Cape of Good Hope, which had to cross the line twice to arrive at its highest perfection. He said that for two years he had been thinking of this gloriously happy day, and had had a ship upon the sea for the purpose of perfecting this wine. He bade the king notice the strangely formed fish, which could only be obtained from the Chinese sea. Then, following up the subject, he spoke of the peculiar and laughable customs and habits of the Chinese, thus causing even the proud queen to laugh at his humorous descriptions.

Count Bruhl was suddenly interrupted in an unusual manner.

His secretary, Willmar, approached the royal table, and without a word of excuse, without greeting the king, handed the count a sealed package!

This was such a crime against courtly etiquette that the count, from sheer amazement, made no excuses to the king; he only cast a threatening look at the secretary. But as he encountered Willmar's pale, terrified countenance, a tremor seized him, and he cast an eager glance upon the papers in his hand, which, no doubt, contained the key to all this mystery. "They are from the commandant at Leipsic," whispered the secretary; "I entreat your excellency to read them."

Before the count had time, however, to open the dispatch, a still stranger event took place.

The Prussian ambassador, who, upon the plea of illness, had declined Count Bruhl's invitation, suddenly appeared in the garden, accompanied by the four secretaries of his legation, and approached the royal table. Upon his countenance there was no sign of sickness, but rather an expression of great joy.

As he neared the tent, the gay song and merry jest ceased. Every eye was fixed inquiringly upon the individual who had dared to disturb this fete by his presence. The music, which had before filled the air with joyous sounds, was now playing a heart-breaking air.

Count Bruhl now arose and advanced. He greeted the Prussian ambassador in a few cold, ceremonious words.

But Count Mattzahn's only answer to this greeting was a silent bow. He then said, in a voice loud enough to be heard by the king and queen:

"Count Bruhl, as ambassador of the King of Prussia, I request you to demand an audience for me at once from the King of Saxony. I have an important dispatch from my king."

Count Bruhl, struck with terror, could only gaze at him, he had not the strength to answer.

But King Augustus, rising from his seat, said:

"The ambassador of my royal brother can approach; I consent to grant him this audience; it is demanded in so strange a manner, it must surely have some important object."

The count entered the royal tent.

"Is it your majesty's wish," said Mattzahn, solemnly, "that all these noble guests shall be witnesses? I am commanded by my royal master to demand a private audience."

"Draw the curtain!" said the king.

Count Bruhl, with trembling fingers, drew the golden cord, and the heavy curtains fell to the ground. They were now completely separated from the guests.

"And now, count," said the king, taking his seat by his proud, silent queen, "speak."

Bowing profoundly, Count Mattzahn drew a dispatch from his pocket, and read in a loud, earnest voice.

It was a manifesto from the King of Prussia, written by himself and addressed to all the European courts. In it, Frederick denied being actuated by any desire of conquest or gain, but declared that he was compelled to commence this war to which Austria had provoked him by her many and prolonged insults. There was a pause when the count finished reading. Upon the gentle, amiable countenance of the king there was now an angry look. The queen was indifferent, cold, and haughty; she seemed to have paid no attention whatever to Count Mattzahn, but, turning to the princess at her side, she asked a perfectly irrelevant question, which was answered in a whisper.

Countess Bruhl dared not raise her eyes; she did not wish her faithless lover, Count Mattzahn, whose cunning political intrigues she now perfectly understood, to see her pain and confusion. The prince-elector, well aware of the importance of this hour, stood at the king's side; behind him was Count Bruhl, whose handsome, sparkling countenance was now deadly pale.

Opposite to this agitated group, stood the Prussian ambassador, whose haughty, quiet appearance presented a marked contrast. His clear, piercing glance rested upon each one of them, and seemed to fathom every thought of their souls. His tall, imposing form was raised proudly, and there was an expression of the noblest satisfaction upon his countenance. After waiting some time in vain for an answer, he placed the manifesto before the king.

"With your majesty's permission, I will now add a few words," said he.

"Speak!" said the king, laconically.

"His majesty, my royal master," continued Count Mattzahn, in a loud voice, "has commissioned me to give your majesty the most quieting assurances, and to convince you that his march through Saxony has no purpose inimical to you, but that he only uses it as a passway to Bohemia."

The king's countenance now became dark and stern, even the queen lost some of her haughty indifference.

"How?" said the king; "Frederick of Prussia does us the honor to pass through our land without permission? He intends coming to Saxony?"

"Sire," said Mattzahn, with a slight smile, "his majesty is already there! Yesterday his army, divided into three columns, passed the Saxon borders!"

The king rose hastily from his seat. The queen was deadly pale, her lips trembled, but she remained silent, and cast a look of bitter hatred upon the ambassador of her enemy.

Count Bruhl was leaning against his chair, trembling with terror, when the king turned to him.

"I ask my prime minister if he knows how far the King of Prussia has advanced into Saxony?"

"Sire, I was in perfect ignorance of this unheard-of event. The King of Prussia wishes to surprise us in a manner worthy of the most skilful magician. Perhaps it is one of those April jests which Frederick II is so fond of practising."

"Your excellency can judge for yourself," said Count Mattzahn, earnestly, "whether the taking of towns and fortresses is to be considered a jest. For, if I am rightly informed, you have this day received two dispatches, informing you of my royal master's line of march."

"How?" said the king, hastily; "you were aware of this, count, and I was not informed? You received important dispatches, and I was not notified of it?"

"It is true," said the count, much embarrassed. "I received two couriers. The dispatches of the first were handed to me the same moment your majesties entered my house; I received the other just as Count Mattzahn arrived. I have, therefore, read neither."

"With your majesty's permission," said Count Mattzahn, "I will inform you of their contents."

"You will be doing me a great service," said the king, earnestly.

"The first dispatch, sire, contained the news that his majesty the King of Prussia had taken without resistance the fortresses of Torgau and Wittenberg!"

A hollow groan escaped the king as he sank in his chair. The queen became paler than before.

"What more?" said the king, gloomily.

"The second dispatch," continued Count Mattzahn, smilingly, "informed his excellency Count Bruhl that the King of Prussia, my noble and victorious master, was pressing forward, and had also taken Leipsic without the slightest resistance!"

"How!" said the king, "he is in Leipsic?"

"Sire, I think he was there," said Count Mattzahn, laughing; "for it seems that the Prussians, led by their king, have taken the wings of the morning. Frederick was in Leipsic when the courier left—he must now be on his way to Dresden. But he has commissioned me to say that his motive for passing through Saxony is to see and request your majesty to take a neutral part in this war between Austria and Prussia."

"A neutral part!" said the king, angrily, "when my land is invaded without question or permission, and peace broken in this inexplicable manner. Have you any other message, count?"

"I have finished, sire, and humbly ask if you have any answer for my sovereign?"

"Tell the king, your master, that I will raise my voice throughout the land of Germany to complain of this unheard-of and arbitrary infringement of the peace. At the throne of the German emperor I will demand by what right the King of Prussia dares to enter Saxony with his army and take possession of my cities. You can depart, sir; I have no further answer for his majesty!"

The count, bowing reverentially to the king and queen, left the royal tent.

Every eye was fixed upon the prime minister. From him alone, who was considered the soul of the kingdom of Saxony, help and counsel was expected. All important questions were referred to him, and all were now eagerly looking for his decision. But the powerful favorite was in despair. He knew how utterly impossible it was to withstand the King of Prussia's army. Every arrangement for this war had been made on paper, but in reality little had been accomplished. The army was not in readiness! The prime minister had been in want of a few luxuries of late, and had, therefore, as he believed there would be no war until the following spring, reduced it. He knew how little Saxony was prepared to battle against the King of Prussia's disciplined troops, and the ambassador's friendly assurances did not deceive him.

"Well, count," said the king, after a long pause, "how is this strange request of Frederick II., that we should remain neutral, to be answered?"

Before the count was able to answer, the queen said, in a loud voice:

"By a declaration of war, my husband! This is due to your honor. We have been insulted; it therefore becomes you to throw down the gauntlet to your presumptuous adversary."

"We will continue this conversation in my apartments," said the king, rising; "this is no place for it. Our beautiful feast has been disturbed in a most brutal manner. Count Bruhl, notify the different ambassadors that, in an hour, I will receive them at my palace."

"This hour is mine!" thought the queen, as she arose; "in it I will stimulate my husband's soft and gentle heart to a brave, warlike decision; he will yield to my prayers and tears." She took the king's arm with a gay smile, and left the tent, followed by the princes, and the host and hostess.

Silently they passed the festive tables, from which the guests had risen to greet them. The courtiers sought to read in their countenances the solution of that riddle which had occupied them since the arrival of the Prussian ambassador, and about which they had been anxiously debating.

But, upon the queen's countenance there was now her general look of indifference. It is true, the king was not smiling as was his wont when amongst his subjects, but his pleasant countenance betrayed no fear or sorrow. The queen maintained her exalted bearing; nothing had passed to bow her proud head. After the royal guests had left, Count Bruhl returned. He also had regained his usual serenity. With ingenious friendliness he turned to his guests, and while requesting them, in a flattering manner, to continue to grace his wife's fete by their presence, demanded for himself leave of absence. Then passing on, he whispered here and there a few words to the different ambassadors. They and the count then disappeared.

The fete continued quietly; the music recommenced its gay, melodious sounds, the birds carolled their songs, and the flowers were as beautiful and as sweet as before. The jewels of the courtiers sparkled as brilliantly. Their eyes alone were not so bright, and the happy smile had left their lips. They were all weighed down by a presentiment that danger was hovering around them.

CHAPTER XIII
THE ARCHIVES AT DRESDEN

Count Mattzahn's prophecy came true. The King of Prussia came to Dresden, and there, as in every other part of Saxony, found no resistance. Fear and terror had gone before him, disarming all opposition. The king and prince-elector were not accustomed to have a will of their own; and Count Bruhl, the favorite of fortune, showed himself weak and helpless in the hour of adversity. It needed the queen's powerful energy, and the forcible representations of the French ambassador, Count Broglio, to arouse them from their lethargy; and what Count Broglio's representations, and the queen's prayers and tears commenced, hatred finished. Count Bruhl's sinking courage rose at the thought of the possibility of still undermining the King of Prussia, and putting an end to his victorious march. It was only necessary to detain him, to prevent him from reaching the Bohemian borders, until the Austrian army came to their assistance, until the French troops had entered and taken possession of Prussia. Therefore, Count Bruhl sent courier after courier to Saxony's allies, to spread her cry for help to every friendly court. He then collected the army, ordered them to camp at Pirna, which was very near the boundary of Bohemia, and, as it was guarded on one side by the Elbe, and on the other by high rocks, appeared perfectly secure. When these preparations were commenced, the count's courage rose considerably, and he determined to prove himself a hero, and to give the Saxon army the inspiring consciousness that, in the hour of danger, their king would be in their midst. The king therefore left for the fortress of Konigstein, accompanied by Count Bruhl, leaving the army, consisting of about seventeen thousand men, to follow under the command of General Rutrosky, and to encamp at the foot of Konigstein. Arrived at Konigstein, where they thought themselves perfectly secure, they gave themselves up to the free and careless life of former days. They had only changed their residence, not their character; their dreams were of future victories, of the many provinces they would take from the King of Prussia; and with this delightful prospect the old gay, luxurious, and wanton life was continued. What difference did it make to Count Bruhl that the army was only provided with commissary stores for fourteen days, and that this time was almost past, and no way had been found to furnish them with additional supplies. The King of Prussia had garrisoned every outlet, and only the King of Saxony's forage-wagon was allowed to pass.

Frederick knew better than the Saxon generals the fearful, invincible enemy that was marching to the camp of Pirna. What were the barricades, the palisades, and ambushes, by which the camp was surrounded, to this enemy? This foe was in the camp, not outside of it—he had no need to climb the barricades—he came hither flying through the air, breathing, like a gloomy bird of death, his horrible cries of woe. This enemy was hunger— enervating, discouraging, demoralizing hunger!

The fourteen days had expired, and in the camp of Pirna languished seventeen thousand men! The bread rations became smaller and smaller; but the third part of the usual meat ration was given; the horses' food also was considerably shortened. Sorrow and starvation reigned in the camp. Why should this distress Count Bruhl? He lived in his usual luxurious splendor, with the king. Looking out from his handsome apartments upon the valley lying at his feet, he saw on a little meadow by which the Elbe was flowing, herds of cows and calves, sheep and beeves, which were there to die like the Saxon soldiers, for their king. These herds were for the royal table; there was, therefore, no danger that the enemy visiting the army should find its way to the fortress. It was also forbidden, upon pain of death, to force one of these animals intended for the royal table, from their noble calling, and to satisfy therewith the hungry soldiers. Count Bruhl could therefore wait patiently the arrival of the Austrian army, which was already in motion, under the command of General Brown.

While the King of Poland was living gay and joyous in the fortress of Konigstein, the queen with the princes of the royal house had remained in Dresden; and though she knew her husband's irresolute character, and knew that the King of Prussia, counting upon this, was corresponding with him, endeavoring to persuade him to neutrality, still she had no fears of her husband succumbing to his entreaties. For was not Count Bruhl, the bitter, irreconcilable enemy of Prussia, at his side?—and had not the king said to her, in a solemn manner, before leaving: "Better that every misfortune come upon us than to take the part of our enemies!" The queen, therefore, felt perfectly safe upon this point. She remained in Dresden for two reasons: first, to watch the King of Prussia, and then to guard the archives—those archives which contained the most precious treasures of Saxon diplomacy—the most important secrets of their allies. These papers were prized more highly by the queen than all the crown jewels now lying in their silver casket; and though the keeping of the latter was given over to some one else, no one seemed brave enough to shield the former. No one but herself should guard these rich treasures. The state archives were placed in those rooms of the palace which had but one outlet, and that leading into one of the queen's apartments. In this room she remained—she took her meals, worked, and slept there—there she received the princes and the foreign ambassadors—always guarding the secret door, of which she carried the key fastened to a gold chain around her neck. But still the queen was continually in fear her treasure would be torn from her, and the King of Prussia's seeming friendliness was not calculated to drive away this anxiety. It is true the king had sent her his compliments by Marshal Keith, with the most friendly assurances of his affection, but notwithstanding this, the chancery, the college, and the mint department had been closed; all the artillery and ammunition had been taken from the Dresden arsenal and carried to Magdeburg; some of the oldest and worthiest officers of the crown had been dismissed; and the Swiss guard, intended for service in the palace, had been disarmed. All this agreed but badly with the king's quieting assurances, and was calculated to increase the hatred of his proud enemy. She had, nevertheless, stifled her anger so far as to invite the King of Prussia, who was staying in the palace of the Countess Morizinska, not far from his army, to her table.

Frederick had declined this invitation. He remained quietly in the palace, whose doors were open to all, giving audience to all who desired it, listening to their prayers, and granting their wishes.

The Queen of Poland heard this with bitter anger; and the more gracious the King of Prussia showed himself to the Saxons, the more furious and enraged became the heart of this princess.

"He will turn our people from their true ruler," said she to Countess Ogliva, her first maid of honor, who was sitting at her side upon a divan placed before the princess's door. "This hypocritical affability will only serve to gain the favor of our subjects, and turn them from their duty."

"It has succeeded pretty well," said the countess, sighing. "The Saxon nobility are continually in the antechamber of this heretical king; and yesterday several of the city authorities, accompanied by the foreign ambassadors, waited upon him, and he received them."

"Yes, he receives every one; he gives gay balls every evening, at which he laughs and jokes merrily. He keeps open house, and the poor people assemble there in crowds to see him eat." Maria Josephine sighed deeply. "I hate this miserable, changeable people!" murmured she.

"And your majesty does well," said the countess, whose wrinkled, yellow countenance was now illuminated by a strange fire. "The anger of God will rest upon this heretical nation that has turned from her salvation, and left the holy mother church in haughty defiance. The King of Poland cannot even appoint true Catholic-Christians as his officers—every position of any importance is occupied by heretics. But the deluge will surely come again upon this sinful people and destroy them."

The queen crossed herself, and prayed in a low voice.

The countess continued: "This Frederick stimulates these heretical Saxons in their wicked unbelief. He, who it is well known, laughs and mocks at every religion, even his own—attended, yesterday, the Protestant church, to show our people that he is a protector of that church."

"Woe, woe to him!" said the queen.

"With listening ear he attended to his so-called preacher's sermon, and then loudly expressed his approval of it, well knowing that this preacher is a favorite of heretics in Dresden. This cunning king wished to give them another proof of his favor. Does your majesty wish to know of the present he made this, preacher?"

"What?" said the queen, with a mocking laugh. "Perhaps a Bible, with the marginal observations of his profligate friends, Voltaire and La Mettrie?"

"No, your majesty; the king sent this learned preacher a dozen bottles of champagne!"

"He is a blasphemous scoffer, even with that which he declares holy. But punishment will overtake him. Already the voice of my exalted nephew, the Emperor of Germany, is to be heard throughout the entire land, commanding the King of Prussia to return at once to his own kingdom, and to make apologies to the King of Poland for his late insults. It is possible that, in his haughty pride, Frederick will take no notice of this command. But it will be otherwise with the generals and commandants of this usurper. They have been commanded by the emperor to leave their impious master, and not to be the sharers of his frightful crime."

"I fear," said Countess Ogliva, sighing, and raising her eyes heavenward—"I fear they will not listen to the voice of our good emperor."

"But they will hear the voice of his cannon," cried the queen, impetuously; "the thunder of our artillery and the anger of God will annihilate them, and they will fall to the ground as if struck by lightning before the swords blessed by our holy priests."

The door of the antechamber was at this moment opened violently, and the queen's chamberlain appeared upon its threshold.

"Your majesty, a messenger from the King of Prussia requests an audience," said he.

The queen's brow became clouded, and she blushed with anger. "Tell this messenger that I am not in a condition to receive his visit, and that he must therefore impart to you his message."

"It is, no doubt, another of his hypocritical, friendly assurances," said the queen, as the chamberlain left. "He has, no doubt, some evil design, and wishes to soothe us before he strikes."

The chamberlain returned, but his countenance was now white with terror.

"Well!" said the queen, "what is this message?"

"Ah, your majesty," stammered the trembling courtier, "my lips would not dare to repeat it; and I could never find the courage to tell you what he demands."

"What he demands!" repeated the queen; "has it come to that, that a foreign prince commands in our land? Go, countess, and in my name, fully empowered by me, receive this King of Prussia's message; then return, and dare not keep the truth from me."

Countess Ogliva and the chamberlain left the royal apartment, and Maria Josephine was alone. And now, there was no necessity of guarding this mask of proud quietude and security. Alone, with her own heart, the queen's woman nature conquered. She did not now force back the tears which streamed from her eyes, nor did she repress the sighs that oppressed her heart. She wept, and groaned, and trembled. But hearing a step in the antechamber, she dried her eyes, and again put on the proud mask of her royalty. It was the countess returning. Slowly and silently she passed through the apartment. Upon her colorless countenance there was a dark, angry expression, and a scoffing smile played about her thin, pale lips.

"The King of Prussia," said she, in a low, whispering voice, as she reached the queen, "demands that the key to the state archives be delivered at once to his messenger, Major von Vangenheim."

The queen raised herself proudly from her seat.

"Say to this Major von Vangenheim that he will never receive this key!" said she, commandingly.

The countess bowed, and left the room.

"He has left," said she, when she returned to the queen; "though he said that he or another would return."

"Let us now consult as to what is to be done," said the queen. "Send for Father Guarini, so that we may receive his advice."

Thanks to the queen's consultation with her confessor and her maid of honor, the King of Prussia's messenger, when he returned, was not denied an audience. This time, it was not Major von Vangenheim, but General von Wylich, the Prussian commandant at Dresden, whom Frederick sent.

Maria Josephine received him in the room next to the archives, sitting upon a divan, near to the momentous door. She listened with a careless indifference, as he again demanded, in the king's name, the key to the state archives.

The queen turned to her maid of honor.

"How is it that you are so negligent, countess?" said she; "did I not tell you to answer to the messenger of the king, that I would give this key, which is the property of the Prince-Elector of Saxony, and which he intrusted to me, to no one but my husband?"

"I had the honor to fulfil your majesty's command," said the countess, respectfully.

"How is it, then," said she, turning to General von Wylich, "that you dare to come again with this request, which I have already answered?"

"Oh, may your majesty graciously pardon me," cried the general, deeply moved; "but his majesty, my king and master, has given me the sternest commands to get the key, and bring him the papers. I am therefore under the sad necessity to beseech your majesty to agree to my master's will."

"Never!" said the queen, proudly. "That door shall never be opened; you shall never enter it."

"Be merciful. I dare not leave here without fulfilling my master's commands. Have pity on my despair, your majesty, and give me the key to that door."

"Listen! I shall not give you the key," said the queen, white and trembling with anger; "and if you open the door by force, I will cover it with my body; and now, sir, if you wish to murder the Queen of Poland, open the door." And raising her proud, imposing form, the queen placed herself before the door.

"Mercy! mercy! queen," cried the general; "do not force me to do something terrible; do not make me guilty of a crime against your sacred royalty. I dare not return to my king without these papers. I therefore implore your majesty humbly, upon my knees, to deliver this key to me."

He fell upon his knees before the queen, humbly supplicating her to repent her decision.

"I will not give it to you," said she, with a triumphant smile. "I do not move from this door; it shall not be opened."

General Wylich rose from his lowly position. He was pale, but there was a resolute expression upon his countenance. Looking upon it, you could not but see that he was about to do something extremely painful to his feelings.

"Queen of Poland," said he, in a loud, firm voice, "I am commanded by my king to bring to him the state archives. Below, at the castle gate, wagons are in attendance to receive them; they are accompanied by a detachment of Prussian soldiers. I have only to open that window, sign to them, and they are here. In the antechamber are the four officers who came with me; by opening the door, they will be at my side."

"What do you mean by this?" said the queen, in a faltering voice, moving slightly from the door.

"I mean, that at any price, I must enter that room. If the key is not given to me, I will call upon my soldiers to break down the door; as they have learned to tear down the walls of a fortress, it will be an easy task; that if the Queen of Poland does not value her high position sufficiently to guard herself against any attack, I will be compelled to lay hands upon a royal princess, and lead her by force from that door, which my soldiers must open! But, once more, I bend my knee, and implore your majesty to preserve me from this crime, and to have mercy on me."

And again he fell upon his knees supplicating for pity.

"Be merciful! be merciful!" cried the queen's confessor and the Countess Ogliva, who both knew that General Wylich would do all that he had said, and had both fallen on their knees, adding their entreaties to his. "Your Majesty has done all that human power can do. It is now time to guard your holy form from insult. Have mercy on your threatened royalty."

"No, no!" murmured the queen, "I cannot! I cannot! Death would be sweet in comparison to this humiliating defeat."

The queen's confessor, Father Guarini, now rose from his knees, and, approaching the queen, he said, in a solemn, commanding voice:

"My daughter, by virtue of my profession, as a servant of the holy mother church, to whom is due obedience and trust, I command you to deliver up to this man the key of this door."

The queen's head fell upon her breast, and hollow, convulsive groans escaped her. Then, with a hasty movement, she severed the key from her chain.

"I obey you, my father," said she. "There is the key, general; this room can now be entered."

General Wylich took the key, kissing reverentially the hand that gave it to him. He then said to her, in a voice full of emotion:

"I have but this last favor to ask of your majesty, that you will now leave this room, so that my soldiers may enter it."

Without answering, the queen, accompanied by her confessor and maid of honor, left the apartment.

"And now," said the queen to Countess Ogliva, as she entered her reception-room, "send messengers at once to all the foreign ambassadors, and tell them I command their presence."

CHAPTER XIV
SAXONY HUMILIATED

A half an hour later the ambassadors of France, Austria, Holland, Russia, and Sweden, were assembled in the queen's reception-room. The queen was there, pale, and trembling with anger. With the proud pathos of misfortune, and humiliated royalty, she apprised them of the repeated insults she had endured, and commanded them to write at once to their different courts, imploring their rulers to send aid to her sorely threatened kingdom.

"And if these princes," said she, impetuously, "help us to battle against this usurper, in defending us they will be defending their own rights and honor. For my cause is now the cause of all kings; for if my crown falls, the foundation of their thrones will also give way. For this little Margrave of Brandenburg, who calls himself King of Prussia, will annihilate us all it we do not ruin him in advance. I, for my part, swear him a perpetual resistance, a perpetual enmity! I will perish willingly in this fight if only my insults are revenged and my honor remains untarnished. Hasten, therefore, to acquaint your courts with all that has occurred here."

"I will be the first to obey your majesty," said the French ambassador, Count Broglio, approaching the queen. "I will repeat your words to my exalted master; I will portray to your majesty's lovely daughter, the Dauphine of France, the sufferings her royal mother has endured, and I know she will strain every nerve to send you aid. With your gracious permission, I will now take my leave, for to-day I start for Paris."

"To Paris!" cried the queen; "would you leave my court in the hour of misfortune?"

"I would be the last to do this, unless forced by necessity," said the count; "but the King of Prussia has just dismissed me, and sent me my passport!"

"Your passport! dismissed you!" repeated the queen. "Have I heard aright? Do you speak of the King of Prussia? Has he then made himself King of Saxony?"

Before anyone had time to answer the queen's painful questions, the door was opened, and the king's ministers entered; beside them was to be seen the pale, terrified countenance of Count Leuke, the king's chamberlain.

Slowly and silently these gentlemen passed through the room and approached the queen.

"We have come," said Count Hoymb, bowing lowly, "to take leave of your majesty."

The queen fell slightly back, and gazed in terror at the four ministers standing before her with bowed heads.

"Has the king, my husband, sent for you? Are you come to take leave of me before starting to Konigstein?"

"No, your majesty; we come because we have been dismissed from our offices by the King of Prussia."

The queen did not answer, but gazed wildly at the sad countenances about her; and now she fixed a searching glance upon the royal chamberlain.

"Well, and you?" said she. "Have you a message for me from my husband? Are you from Konigstein?"

"Yes, your majesty, I come from Konigstein. But I am not a bearer of pleasant news. I am sent to Dresden by the King of Poland to request of the King of Prussia passports for himself and Count Bruhl. The king wishes to visit Warsaw, and is therefore desirous of obtaining these passports."

"Ah!" said the queen, sighing, "to think that my husband requires permission to travel in his own kingdom, and that he must receive it from our enemy! Well, have you obeyed the king's command, Count Leuke? Have you been to the King of Prussia and received the passports?"

"I was with the King of Prussia," said the count, in a faltering voice.

"Well, what more?"

"He refused me! He does not give his consent to this visit."

"Listen, listen!" said the queen, wildly; "hear the fresh insult thrown at our crown! Can God hear this and not send His lightning to destroy this heretical tyrant? Ah, I will raise my voice; it shall be a cry of woe and lamentation, and shall resound throughout all Europe; it shall reach every throne, and every one shall hear my voice calling out: 'Woe! woe! woe to us all; our thrones are tottering, they will surely fall if we do not ruin this evil-doer who threatens us all!'"

With a fearful groan, the queen fell fainting into the arms of Countess Ogliva. But the sorrows and humiliations of this day were not the only ones experienced by Maria Josephine from her victorious enemy.

It is true her cry for help resounded throughout Europe. Preparations for war were made in many places, but her allies were not able to prevent the fearful blow that was to be the ruin of Saxony. Though the Dauphine of France, daughter of the wretched Maria Josephine, and the mother of the unfortunate King of France, Louis XVI., threw herself at the feet of Louis XV., imploring for help for her mother's tottering kingdom, the French troops came too late to prevent this disaster. Even though Maria Theresa, Empress of Austria, and niece to the Queen of Saxony, as her army were in want of horses, gave up all her own to carry the cannon. The Austrian cannon was of as little help to Saxony as the French troops.

Starvation was a more powerful ally to Prussia than Austria, France, Russia, and Sweden were to Saxony, for in the Saxon camp also a cry of woe resounded.

It was hunger that compelled the brave Saxon General Rutrosky to capitulate. It was the same cause that forced the King of Saxony to bind himself to the fearful stipulations which the victorious King of Prussia, after having tried in vain for many years to gain an ally in Saxony, made.

In the valley of Lilienstein the first of that great drama, whose scenes are engraved in blood in the book of history, was performed, and for whose further developments many sad, long years were necessary.

In the valley of Lilienstein the Saxon army, compelled to it by actual starvation, gave up their arms; and as these true, brave soldiers, weeping over their humiliation, with one hand laid down their weapons, the other was extended toward their enemies for bread.

Lamentation and despair reigned in the camp at Lilienstein, and there, at a window of the castle of Konigstein, stood the Prince-Elector of Saxony, with his favorite Count Bruhl, witnesses to their misery.

After these fearful humiliations, by which Frederick punished the Saxons for their many intrigues, by which he revenged himself for their obstinate, enmity, their proud superiority—after these humiliations, after their complete defeat, the King of Prussia was no longer opposed to the King of Saxony's journey. He sent him the desired passports, he even extended their number, and not only sent one to the king and to Count Bruhl, but also to the Countess Bruhl, with the express command to accompany her husband. He also sent a pass to Countess Ogliva, compelling this bigoted woman to leave her mistress.

And when the queen again raised her cry of woe, to call her allies to her aid, the King of Prussia answered her with the victorious thunder of the battle of Losovitz, the first battle fought in this war, and in which the Prussians, led by their king, performed wonders of bravery, and defeated for the third time the tremendous Austrian army, under the command of General Brown.

"Never," says Frederick, "since I have had the honor to command the Prussian troops, have they performed such deeds of daring as to-day."

The Austrians, in viewing these deeds, cried out:

"We have found again the old Prussians!"

And still they fought so bravely, that the Prussians remarked in amazement: "These cannot be the same Austrians!"

This was the first act of that great drama enacted by the European nations, and of which King Frederick II. was the hero.